Prescription: Romance™

"Do you have a twin?"

Mariah asked, trying to reconcile this man with the one she'd met earlier.

Physically he resembled the same Andrew Prescott who'd stridden into the Winding Trails Inn. He wore the same clothes, possessed the same rugged features she considered intriguing, and combed his hair in the same manner.

Emotionally, however, his attitude was as far removed as the North Pole was from the South, and she struggled not to take his chilly reception personally.

Jessica Matthews's interest in medicine began at a young age, and she nourished it with medical stories and hospital-based television programs. After a stint as a teenage candy striper, she pursued a career as a clinical laboratory scientist. When not writing, or on duty, she fills her day with countless family and school-related activities. Jessica lives in the central United States with her husband, daughter and son.

Prescription: Romance™

DR. PRESCOTT'S DILEMMA
JESSICA MATTHEWS

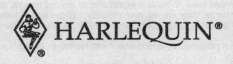

HARLEQUIN®

TORONTO • NEW YORK • LONDON
AMSTERDAM • PARIS • SYDNEY • HAMBURG
STOCKHOLM • ATHENS • TOKYO • MILAN • MADRID
PRAGUE • WARSAW • BUDAPEST • AUCKLAND

ISBN 0-373-83380-6

DR. PRESCOTT'S DILEMMA

First North American Publication 1998.

CHAPTER ONE

'WHAT do you mean, you don't have a room? I made a reservation.' Mariah Henning dug the typed confirmation letter out of her voluminous shoulder-bag and placed it on the counter. 'This *is* the Winding Trails Inn of Gallup, Wyoming, isn't it?'

The motel clerk, a man in his mid-sixties, gave the paper a cursory glance and shrugged. 'It is, but we're full up. Rodeo started this past weekend so folks have been coming to town in droves. Best I can do is offer you something in a coupla days.'

Mariah took a deep breath, feeling her shoulders slump. For the last thirty miles of her journey she'd dangled the image of a refreshing shower in front of her, like a handful of sugar cubes before a mare with a sweet tooth. Knowing she had a long trip ahead of her, she'd taken few pains with her appearance before she'd left North Platte early this morning. There had seemed to be little point in wearing an uncomfortable business suit for a three-hour car ride, only to arrive both tired and wrinkled.

She'd never dreamed, however, that the room she'd reserved at the end of her journey would be unavailable. There simply had to be a mistake.

'I have your confirmation letter,' she repeated. 'For June twenty-third. One night. That's today. See?'

He studied the page. 'Yup, but I don't have a room. Not until Friday.'

'Then why did you send me this notice?'

Once again he shrugged. 'I'm just looking after the desk so's my son can be at the rodeo. You'll have to take up the mistake with him or his wife.'

'When will they be back?'

'Can't say for sure.'

'Are there any other motels in town?' she asked.

He nodded. 'They're full, too.'

Desperation reared its head. Her meeting with the human resources director of Gallup Memorial Hospital was crucial. She couldn't attend wearing shorts and a Mickey Mouse T-shirt stained from her mishap with a can of cola.

She'd already been briefed by other TLC Inc representatives who'd tried to obtain Gallup Memorial's business. They'd reported a receptive welcome by most members of this organization, but Dr Andrew Prescott— a physician with obvious clout—had been hard to convince. Consequently, this hospital's patronage had slipped through their proverbial fingers time after time.

Mariah had encouraged her boss and TLC Inc owner, Glenn Howell, to cut his losses and seek other prospective clients. Failure, however, wasn't part of Glenn's vocabulary. Instead, he'd sent Mariah to achieve the impossible, promising her a promotion if she obtained the coveted contract.

To that end, however, if she wanted to convince the parties involved of her company's professionalism, she had to look the part. Without a room to recharge her energy, review her notes and freshen her wilted appearance she faced an impossible task.

'How far to the next motel?' she asked.

'Forty-five miles.'

She brushed at her fringe on her forehead. There was only one alternative and, considering what was at stake, she had to take it. 'Look,' she began, trying not to sound as desperate as she felt. 'I have an important meeting in an hour and half. Do you have a public library?' She'd find a quiet corner, relax and then change in the restroom.

The old man nodded. 'Other side of Ziggy's gas station. Go down the street two blocks, take a right, then a left. Can't miss it. It's before you get to McDonald's.'

The mention of the famous fast-food restaurant reminded her of how long it had been since her Danish and orange juice. She changed her agenda to move lunch to the top of her priority list.

'Thanks,' she said politely, although inwardly she grumbled. Having spent most of the last three months wandering through Wyoming, Colorado, Nebraska and Kansas in search of new clients and prospective employees, she was tired of travelling.

'So, do you want a room for tomorrow night?' he asked.

Her answer was swift and sure. 'No.' Although she'd planned on driving to Denver in the morning after she'd rested, the thought of arriving in her own condominium and sleeping in her own queen-sized bed banished most of her irritation. Armed with a Thermos of strong coffee and a radio blaring rock music, she should pull into her personal parking stall by midnight.

The door squeaked and a man in his mid-thirties entered. His alert expression, firm strides and squared shoulders spoke of responsibility and authority. He clearly was a person who didn't accept or tolerate half-measures from anyone, including himself.

A few strands of silver highlighted the neatly parted straight coffee-coloured hair. His hunter green trousers possessed a razor-sharp crease and his short-sleeved green-and-blue plaid cotton shirt appeared without spot or wrinkle.

After removing his sunglasses, he tucked one stem into the breast pocket of his shirt. While he did so she studied his features. He wasn't a handsome man by the world's standards—his face possessed a rugged Lincolnesque quality that she found intriguing—but his brown eyes were warm and friendly and matched the smile he bestowed upon her.

As she returned his infectious grin she summed him up as a prime specimen of health and vitality. Unfortunately, she couldn't say the same for herself. With her hair windblown, her face devoid of make-up, her forehead and nose glistening with a sheen of perspiration, she felt decidedly unkempt.

'If you change your mind, let me know.' The elderly man sounded unconcerned.

For a split second she stared at him in disbelief. How could he think she'd be here tomorrow if she didn't have a place to spend the night? As a college student some fifteen years ago, she wouldn't have batted an eye at sleeping in her car and had, in fact, done so on one unforgettable occasion with her girlfriends. But she was older and wiser now, and far less apt to throw caution to the wind.

'Thanks, but I won't be here.' Considering their conversation ended, she turned toward the door. Before she took a step the clerk addressed the man who'd arrived.

'Howdy, Drew. What can I do for you today?'

'Hi, Burt. Steve's laying my carpet today and the house is in a shambles. I thought I'd see if you had a vacancy. Just for tonight.'

His baritone captivated her. The deep pitch seemed to reverberate through the room and settle inside her being.

Chiding herself for her fanciful thoughts, she reached for the doorknob and smirked. You're out of luck, mister, she thought, pulling the door open.

'No problem,' Burt answered cheerfully. 'Just a minute. I'll get you a key.'

No problem? Mariah froze. After a precise military pivot, she marched to the desk before the door slammed.

'Excuse me,' she said in a polite but firm voice, 'a minute ago you didn't have a room available. Now you do?'

'Drew delivered my grandson and fixed up my gall bladder. I wouldn't dream of turning down one of his requests.' Burt appeared affronted at the idea.

'Fine, but *I* had a reservation. Dated three weeks ago,' she reminded him.

Drew spoke. 'Is there a problem?'

The old man's set jaw and narrowed eyes made her think of a stray dog, defending his personal territory. No matter what she said or did her arguments would be futile. If Burt had to choose between a stranger and a local—more specifically, his beloved family physician—'Doctor Drew' would win by a landslide.

To add insult to injury, if she wanted Gallup Memorial's business, she couldn't afford to alienate one of the staff. Small towns protected their own, and if she complained she'd never convince the hospital's management to utilize her agency. Doctors tended to manipulate events to suit themselves. It was all part of their god complex.

The words she swallowed formed a bitter knot in her throat. 'No,' she said quietly, holding Burt's gaze until he capitulated and glanced away. 'A misunderstanding. That's all.'

After delivering her rejoinder, she fled from the room

as if a swarm of bees chased after her. She stomped towards her Toyota Corolla, ignoring the unladylike thud of her trainers against the cracked sidewalk. Her temples throbbed and her face seemed as hot as the air rising off the paved street.

The sound of children laughing and water splashing came from a distance. Tempting though it was to take an invigorating dip in the public pool, she didn't have time. Her mood grew darker.

She tried to insert the key into the lock, but either anger, low blood sugar or both caused a trembling she couldn't control. Leaning against the car, she released a deep sigh before she jabbed at the thin hole once again.

Without warning, a large hand covered hers and stilled her jerky movements. Startled, she glanced up to see the doctor, a serious expression on his face.

'I'm sorry for the confusion, Miss Henning,' he said. 'Burt explained the situation.'

Her thoughts scattered under Drew's lingering touch. It took her a few seconds to collect them. 'He did?'

'Yes, and now I feel guilty.' His smile was apologetic.

'It wasn't your fault.'

'Not directly, perhaps. But I contributed to the situation.' He peered at her as he loosened his hold on her. 'You're not from around here.'

'No.'

'What will you do if you can't find a room?' He perched his Oakleys on the bridge of his nose in one smooth motion.

She shrugged, minimizing her disappointment at having to forego a night's sleep before she returned to Interstate 80. 'I'll drive home. To Denver,' she clarified, shielding her eyes from the sun to stare at him.

'A long trip,' he commented.

'Yes, well, a person has to do what a person has to do.' She didn't mean to come across as curt, but she did.

He lifted her right hand. Before she realized what he was doing he had dropped a long piece of metal into her palm—metal warmed by his own skin.

She stared at the key, which looked like a museum piece, *circa* 1890. 'What's this for?'

'To open your room. Number ten.'

'My room?' she asked dumbly. 'I don't have one.'

'You do now. Enjoy the accommodation with my compliments.'

Mariah shook her head. 'I can't accept this.'

He reached out and closed her fingers around the object. 'Yes, you can. You had a reservation and I didn't.'

'But Burt—'

'Knows what I'm doing.'

'But where will *you* sleep?' She could easily imagine him, lying in bed with dark sheets gathered at his waist, his chest bare with a sprinkling of hair and his arms tucked behind his head in a pose of utter relaxation.

The idea sent another wave of heat to her face. If she was lucky, he'd attribute her rising colour to being in the sun rather than to racy thoughts.

He shrugged. 'I've spent the night on a cot in the hospital before. I can do it again.'

'Then *I'll* feel guilty.'

His infectious grin grew wide. 'A doctor's got to do what a doctor's got to do.'

Her mouth curved into a smile that was equally broad. 'Tough life, isn't it?'

'We can't have visitors leave Gallup with a bad opinion,' he said. As if he'd sensed her reluctance, he turned her to face the right-hand side of the motel complex. 'Room ten is that way.' He pointed.

She glanced over her shoulder at him, somewhat stunned by her sudden good fortune. 'Thanks.'

With a jaunty salute he wheeled, then climbed into the freshly washed black Land Cruiser parked beside her Corolla. An instant later he reversed out of the stall and left her staring at the gleaming chrome rear bumper.

What a nice man, she thought, wishing for a way to return the favour. In the next instant, however, her sluggish mind pieced together the clues she'd been given.

The friendly Drew who'd reportedly delivered Burt's grandchild had to be the reportedly uncooperative Dr Andrew Prescott. Gallup was too small a community to have two physicians with names so similar.

She opened her fingers and glanced at the key lying on her palm. In spite of the horror stories circulating among TLC's management team, she'd glimpsed a previously unseen side to Dr Prescott. Her woman's intuition gave her a feeling of peace about the upcoming meeting.

She was off to a good start.

Mariah couldn't believe she'd been so wrong.

After showering, changing to her blue serge business suit and braiding her hair, she'd felt ready to tackle anything. Staring into Andrew Prescott's stony face as they exchanged a handshake in Gary Wright's office less than two hours later, her confidence wavered. His dark eyes were remote, his smile absent. His posture reminded her of a mountain lion on the prowl with her as his quarry.

'Ms Henning,' he acknowledged. His former velvety baritone now sounded cold and gruff.

'Dr Prescott,' she returned, as she tried to reconcile the traits of the man before her with the one she'd met earlier. 'It's nice to see you again.'

Gary appeared startled. 'You two know each other?'

'We met,' Andrew said. 'But we weren't introduced.' His pointed glance at Mariah made her feel as if he held her responsible for the oversight. At the same time, she received a distinct impression that had he known her identity he would never have relinquished his motel room to her.

'Do you have a twin?' she asked, trying to reconcile this man with the one she'd met earlier.

Physically, he resembled the same Andrew Prescott who'd stridden into the Winding Trails Inn. He wore the same trousers and shirt, possessed the same rugged features she considered intriguing, and combed his hair in the same manner.

Emotionally, however, his attitude was as far removed as the North Pole was from the South. Underneath his polite demeanour she detected an emotion she couldn't quite identify. Hostility seemed too strong a word. Distrust perhaps, even wariness, with a dose of resentment thrown in for good measure.

Gary chuckled. 'The single women of this town would be delighted if Andrew *did* have a twin.'

Andrew shot him a glare, clearly irritated by the other man's humour. 'Can we get on with this?'

She struggled not to take his chilly reception personally. She'd encountered scepticism from medical providers on other occasions and had been warned by her colleagues about Dr Prescott. From the stubborn set of his jaw and the muscle tensing in his cheek, to persuade him of TLC's professionalism wouldn't be an easy task. It would require every ounce of her negotiating skill.

Her stomach tightened into a knot and she tensed at the challenge facing her.

'Yes, of course.' Gary moved to the executive chair

behind his desk, while Mariah accepted one of the two seats strategically placed in front of it.

She glanced in Andrew's direction. His face was impassive but, as if he'd felt her scrutiny, he met her gaze, steepled his fingers and raised one sardonic brow.

Mariah laid her briefcase on her lap, careful to keep the hem of her skirt below her knees. The latches clicked open with a snap, then she removed a handful of glossy leaflets and began passing them to the two men.

'These are our updated brochures. They contain comprehensive information about our agency, including the services we provide, the screening process for our employees and so on. I'm sure you've heard this story from our previous representatives.'

Gary nodded. Andrew's silence and poker face unnerved her. She continued. 'We pride ourselves on the calibre of our staff. We don't hire applicants with questionable backgrounds any more than our clients would. People are our business, and if we can't offer you the very best we've defeated our purpose.'

Andrew closed his brightly coloured pamphlet. 'Let's cut right to the chase. I want to hear about the support service personnel you claim to provide.'

His cynicism didn't pass unnoticed, but she ignored it for the time being. 'In the last year we've made a concerted effort to expand in fields other than nursing— namely, respiratory therapy, the laboratory and radiology.'

'We're well aware of those efforts,' he said curtly.

He was? Mariah mentally ran through the most recent job fairs. As far as she could remember none had been in the area. She glanced at Gary for a clue and was puzzled by his reaction. Adjusting his tie, he appeared

uncomfortable, as if expecting an explosion and waiting
for it to happen.

Mariah addressed Andrew. 'As I stated earlier, we
only select qualified individuals who have met all the
local and national certification requirements pertaining
to their profession.'

Dr Prescott skewered her with his gaze. 'Right now,
Ms Henning, we're in desperate need of a laboratory
person. Can you meet that need?'

'Yes.'

'Within the forty-eight hours, as stated in your brochure?'

Mariah mentally reviewed her staffing list. One
woman would end her contract on Friday. Others would
complete their obligations in the coming weeks. 'At this
point, everyone is contracted. Monday would be the
soonest I'd have a tech available.'

'Not good enough.'

'Since we couldn't meet our guarantee, you'd receive
her services for the first week at a reduced rate—'

He interrupted, shaking his head. 'Not good enough,'
he repeated. 'If you want my vote you'll have to honour
your own terms. I don't want to wait five days—I want
someone *now*.'

Two realizations hit her at once. Although she'd tried
to give him the benefit of the doubt, her favourable opinion of Andrew Prescott died a swift but painful death.
Secondly, the cost of landing this account seemed terribly high. She didn't want a partnership because of
money or the prestige it brought—she wanted it because
of the frantic pace it provided. In any event, her alter-
natives were limited. Lose this account or provide the
only person who could step into the position on such
short notice.

She fortified herself with a bracing breath. Her boss wouldn't mind what she was about to do since it would achieve his goal. 'You'll have someone.'

His eyes widened slightly, as if he hadn't expected her to meet his demand. She'd clearly foiled his plan. 'I thought you didn't have anyone available?'

She shrugged. 'I was mistaken.'

He leaned forward. 'Who?'

'Me.' Her other responsibilities flitted through her mind. Keeping contact with her subordinates, arranging schedules and dealing with a myriad other details would still rest upon her shoulders, but with computers and faxes she should be able to handle those reins as well— at least until someone was free to take over this position.

'You?'

She nodded. 'I'm a qualified tech.'

He shook his head and leaned back. 'You're totally unacceptable.'

Her hackles rose at his rejection. 'Why? I have a four-year college degree and a year of the required lab internship. I worked at Denver General for five years, National Jewish for three and TLC Inc for the last two. I've also maintained my certification through continuing education.' She paused in her recitation. 'Do you have a problem with my credentials or my experience?'

'No, but I'll expect you to remain until we can hire a permanent replacement. Nancy doesn't have time to train someone new every other week.'

So much for her idea to fill in until one of the other techs could step into this slot.

'Once we place a temp he or she is yours for the duration,' she said. 'Provided, of course, the individual doesn't have a family emergency.' She watched his gaze move to her hands. Although she wanted to twist the ring around her finger, as was her habit when nervous, she clasped her hands together and rested them on top of the briefcase.

'Do you anticipate any family emergencies, *Ms* Henning?'

He was obviously curious about her private life, but a combination of stubbornness and pique prevented her from relating the details.

'No.'

He raised one eyebrow in disbelief. To her relief he didn't press her further.

'For my own information,' she asked, 'what's the time frame involved?'

Andrew glanced at Gary. 'Not long. Six months, give or take.'

Her breath caught in her throat. *Six months?* At this rate, she wouldn't get home for more than a brief visit until the end of the year. Then again, when she'd accepted TLC's offer, travelling had been part of the job description. Even if the position hadn't sounded intriguing, that fact alone had played a major role in her decision to leave the hospital where she and Dave had worked.

She crossed her fingers. 'No problem. Of course, you must provide housing.'

'I expected as much,' Gary admitted. 'My secretary is working on it even as we speak. I assume you have a contract to sign?'

'Yes.' Once again Mariah withdrew a sheaf of papers from her briefcase.

Gary perused the document. Silence descended like a heavy blanket, broken only by the scratch of his pen against the pages. After returning a copy to her, he got to his feet, his face wreathed in smiles.

'Now that we have that settled,' he said a trifle too heartily, 'Drew can show you the lab.'

'Thank you.' She rose to shake Gary's hand, before turning toward Andrew. Although he, too, had come to his feet his arms were folded across his chest and his expression hadn't softened.

'Ready?'

Hearing his impatient tone, she pasted a smile on her face and used her most confident-sounding voice. 'Yes, thank you.' Deep inside, however, she wasn't as certain. She couldn't imagine anything worse than spending time alone with someone who'd rather escort her to the nearest exit and lock the door behind her.

If she only knew why.

She fell into step beside him. As they entered the maze of corridors she tried to fix various landmarks in her mind, wondering if the hospital's architects had forgotten that the shortest distance between two points was a straight line. On the other hand, perhaps her guide merely wanted to confuse her with a circuitous route.

In one hallway the foot traffic became heavy. Two staff members, their patient on a gurney, careened past in an obvious hurry to reach their destination. To avoid becoming a casualty, she moved out of the way and brushed against Andrew's arm in the process.

He stiffened.

'Excuse me,' she murmured, putting space between them as soon as the hallway had cleared.

A pair of nurses met them, both fortyish and wearing pastel-print scrub suits. 'Good afternoon, Dr Prescott,' they said in unison.

'Ladies,' he replied, his face relaxing into a grin reminiscent of the one he'd bestowed upon her at the motel.

A few seconds later his features resettled into their former harsh lines.

She lengthened her stride to match his—a difficult task, made worse by her heeled pumps. 'It looks like I won't need your room any more. I'll leave the key at the desk.'

'Fine.'

Mariah felt hurt and insulted. Working with Andrew Prescott over the next few months would be impossible if he couldn't be congenial. Battlegrounds weren't her style.

Irritated by his attitude, she stopped in her tracks. 'Dr Prescott!'

He stopped and turned, raising one eyebrow. 'Yes?'

She deliberately moved closer until she stood toe to toe with him. 'I don't know why you have such a dislike of me, but I refuse to be treated like a pariah. I won't tolerate rudeness, even from a physician. You weren't like this when I met you.'

A muscle tensed in his jaw. 'At the time I didn't know who you were.'

'I'm the same person now that I was a few hours ago. I deserve an explanation for your hostility.'

'You're right. You might as well know, since I haven't kept my feelings secret, I don't like temporary agencies. Yours in particular.'

She felt as if she'd been slapped. 'Why? We've never placed anyone here before. How could you feel that way?'

His steely-eyed gaze matched hers. 'Firms like yours milk hospitals for everything you can get. We pay a premium price for a warm body, not to mention the housing, vacation and sick leave.'

'If you didn't like the financial terms of the contract

you didn't have to accept them. Negotiation is the name of the game. You should have said something.'

'I couldn't.' He motioned to an intersecting hallway. 'Turn left.'

She complied. 'Why not?'

'Because we're desperate.' His words were delivered slowly and with emphasis. 'If we don't find someone to help Nancy she's threatened to quit. A hospital can't operate without a laboratory.'

'In that case, I'd think you'd be grateful for what TLC Inc can do for you.'

He gave her a look of total disdain. 'Not when I hold you responsible for the situation.'

Her mouth fell open. 'You do? Why?'

'A year ago you created the very vacancy you're filling. Poetic justice, isn't it?'

'How?' she demanded.

'I'm referring to Kelly Evers, leaving us for your organization.'

Kelly? Kelly had grown up in Gallup? Mariah tried to hide her surprise and failed.

'Then you know her?' he asked.

'Not well, but, yes, I know her. She *is* one of our staff.' Her sixth sense told her that now wasn't a good time to admit that she'd thrown the young woman a baby shower. She decided to take the offensive.

'Do you hold a grudge against every person who leaves your employ?'

'No. I'm waging a personal protest at your recruiting tactics. Your agency lures medical personnel away from small communities who struggle to attract and retain professionals.'

'We don't *lure* our employees. We also don't seek

them out and no one forces them to sign on as a temporary. It's strictly their decision.'

'How many of them base their decision on unrealistic expectations?'

'We don't promise anything.'

Andrew shook his head. 'I disagree. Your brochure is a prime example. You portray a world of glamour with your pictures of cruise ships and exotic locales.'

'Of course we present ourselves in a good light,' she said a trifle waspishly. 'While we've placed a few of our nurses in such situations, we certainly don't promise the same opportunity to everyone. You can't blame people for wanting to search out new experiences. Explore life, if you will.'

'And what happens to those left behind while the ones they depend on are off "exploring"?'

He grabbed her left hand and held it aloft. 'How does your husband feel about you being gone? Don't you have an obligation to him, or is he content to see you one weekend a month?'

Tears pricked behind Mariah's eyelids and a familiar ache began to build in her chest. She swallowed hard. Squaring her shoulders, she wrenched her hand free as she met his gaze unflinchingly.

'Your powers of observation are failing, Doctor. This isn't a wedding ring. It's an engagement ring.'

'A matter of semantics. Is he willing to conduct a long-distance romance? Is that how it's done these days?'

She held firm under his gaze. 'No, it's not, but my personal life doesn't concern you.'

'It does if you can't fulfil your part of the contract.'

She spoke in her most haughty manner. 'If the contract is broken, it won't be on my account.'

'No week-long trips home to plan the "event of the century"?' Sarcasm dripped from his words.

She should have known he wouldn't be happy unless he delved into the part of her life that she'd been trying so hard for the past two years to put behind her. Few people knew the circumstances, not because there was anything shameful but because she grew tired of the reactions she received. Pity was the one she hated. Being told to forget Dave and move on with her life irritated her.

How could she forget the one man who'd meant everything to her? How could she replace him in her affections as easily as she replaced a broken test tube?

Dr Prescott obviously wouldn't let up until he'd received the sought-after information. She swallowed hard.

'I'm not making any wedding plans so there won't be any "event of the century",' she said quietly. 'The reason is, I don't have a prospective groom.'

A furrow appeared on his forehead. 'No fiancé?'

'Not any more.' Considering how much the subject pained her, she was proud of her composure.

'Why not?'

'Because he's dead.'

[faint reversed show-through text at top of page]

CHAPTER TWO

MARIAH'S announcement hung in the air like a cloud of thick smoke, saturating Andrew with instant remorse. Rarely at a loss for words, he found himself speechless.

The pain in Mariah's eyes sent a wave of guilt coursing through him. By the time his tongue began to work again she had lifted her chin in regal disdain.

'If you also want to blame me for ozone depletion and the escalating tensions in the Middle East, go right ahead. To be honest, I'm flattered that you think I wield such far-reaching control. However, I refuse to bear the brunt of your anger toward Miss Evers. If she sampled some of what you're dishing out to me, I can certainly understand why she'd leave Gallup.

'Now, if you'll excuse me, I have work to do.'

She stomped past, leaving him behind. He didn't blame her. If he'd endured someone's surly manner and caustic remarks he'd have reacted in the same manner.

He hurried to catch up, then fell into step beside her. 'I'm sorry,' he said, wincing at his stiff tone and the words that seemed trite. 'I didn't have any right to question your personal life.'

She didn't glance at him, but kept her attention focused directly ahead. Obviously her temper still simmered and she wouldn't let him off the hook so easily for his rudeness. 'No, you didn't.'

'I apologize—'

'Save it.' Her heels made dull thuds on the low-pile carpeting. 'I don't want your insincere platitudes.'

'I'm serious,' he protested.

She shook her head. 'There isn't anything you could say at this moment to convince me otherwise. You've said enough in our short acquaintance and I refuse to listen to any more. Right now, my only concern lies in how my agency can help Gallup Memorial.'

A sign on the wall loomed ahead. LABORATORY, it read, with an arrow pointing directly ahead. She quickened her pace but he adjusted his stride to accommodate it. He hated unfinished business and he intended to resolve this matter before they reached their destination.

'Can we stop a minute?' he asked, grabbing her elbow.

She complied without a word.

Before he could offer another apology the beeper on his belt chirped. Muttering under his breath at the untimely interruption, he read the message. 'I have to go to the ER.'

'Fine.'

'Can you find your way?'

She pointed to another sign posted on the wall to her right. 'I *am* able to read.'

'I'll check on you later.'

'Suit yourself.' She walked on without a backward glance and left Andrew to stare at her, feeling a combination of disbelief and irritation.

She had to be the most infuriating woman he'd ever met. He'd tried to make amends and she'd had the audacity to accuse him of insincerity.

Wouldn't you if the roles were reversed?

The thought came from nowhere and pierced his conscience as he retraced his steps to the ER. He had come across as unbending and unyielding, and would plead guilty to those charges.

Part of his reaction had stemmed from his surprise at seeing her in Gary's office. Dressed in her royal blue business suit with her cinnamon-coloured hair tamed into a neat braid, she'd seemed unapproachable and self-sufficient—a complete change from the young woman who'd appeared at the motel exhausted and in need of a helping hand.

At their initial meeting he'd been entranced by her high forehead, elfin nose and perfectly formed mouth. And somehow her long hair had suddenly seemed so...so...*feminine*. He'd wondered at the time if her personality contained the same fiery spark that ran through her tresses. Now he had his answer. It did.

The texture of her soft skin had lingered in his mind all morning. He could still feel the imprint of her small bones in his large palm and, although he tried, he couldn't shake that particular memory.

As he rounded a corner he knew what lay at the crux of the matter. Exasperation. He didn't want to see the human side of the woman he'd labelled as a barracuda. He also didn't want to experience the strong pull of attraction towards that same woman.

Unfortunately, he did both.

Earlier in the day he'd entertained notions of returning to room ten at the motel after his office closed. He didn't like to eat alone and he'd hoped the elusive woman would be interested in joining him. The dark circles under her eyes had raised his curiosity and aroused his protective instincts.

No one came to Gallup by accident. It was too far off the beaten path to attract even the most hopelessly lost traveller. Since Burt had mentioned something about a meeting, Andrew had assumed her arrival had been tied to the rumours of a western clothing factory, relocating to their county. He didn't like being wrong.

He sighed, recognizing another unwanted emotion tugging at him—sympathy. If the pain in her eyes provided any indication, she hadn't come to terms with the unfinished business in her life. Having assumed the role of 'problem-solver' in his relationships, he fought the urge to perform the same function for Mariah Henning. She had her problems; he had his. Unfortunately, his main one was linked to her.

He raked one hand through his hair. A year on, annoyance over Kelly's abrupt departure still gnawed at him. His plans to attract new physicians depended on the support given by critical areas of the hospital. Without Kelly the lab section had fallen apart. Retaining personnel was their number-one problem.

Perhaps if she'd voiced her unhappiness the news wouldn't have hit him so hard. From the moment she'd met Mariah Henning Kelly's personality had changed to the point where she'd been eager to leave her ailing mother in favour of a footloose life.

Mariah's employment at Gallup Memorial seemed the ultimate in adding insult to injury. Unless she was grossly negligent she would be here for a while. Although he couldn't change the past, he would do his best to ensure that Ms Henning thought twice about recruiting her staff from small town facilities.

Armed with a new plan of attack, he strode through the ER door. 'What do we have, Bonnie?' he asked the nurse behind the desk.

'Clint Spaulding's boy, Travis. Animal bite.'

'One of theirs?'

'No. A stray dog.'

His stomach clenched into a knot of fear for his godchild and his parents. Living on a ranch—*his* ranch—he knew the risks of wild animals wandering on the land. 'Did they capture the dog?'

'I don't know. I checked and we have a supply of the rabies vaccine on hand.'

He sent a silent wish heavenward. 'I hope we won't need it.'

'Me too.'

In the exam room he found Clint's wife, Karen, holding the five-year-old tow-headed Travis on her lap. The boy's red T-shirt and blue jeans streaked with dirt and grass stains reflected his love for the outdoors. Someone had rolled his pants leg up to his knee and had pulled off a shoe, leaving a dusty white sock on his foot. His child-sized black cowboy boot stood on the floor next to Karen's chair.

'What's up, cowpoke?' Drew joked.

'Gotted bit.' Travis's lower lip trembled. A trail of tears had dried on his cherubic face.

'Sorry to bother you at the hospital instead of your office,' Karen said. 'Your receptionist encouraged us to come to the ER as you were already here.'

'I'm glad you did.' He bent over to examine Travis's calf. A circular area several inches in diameter was bruised and exhibited several puncture marks that corresponded with canine incisors. A jagged tear marred a section of skin several inches long.

'What happened, Trav?'

Travis brushed at his eyes. 'Was outside playin' wif my trucks in my sandpile. This brown dog came up to me. Since he was so purty, I tried to pet him. But he growled at me.'

Karen brushed wisps of dark hair away from her face. 'I'd glanced through the window and saw a strange collie in the yard. The next thing I knew, Trav started screaming. Blood was running down his leg and he was limping. I called for Clint, but by the time he got to the house the dog had disappeared.'

'Did Clint see which direction it went?'

Her lower lip trembled. 'I didn't stay long enough to find out.'

'It's possible the dog's rabid,' Andrew said gently.

'I know.' Her smile was tremulous. 'Maybe he's someone's lost pet,' she finished on a hopeful note.

'Let's hope so. If not, we'll have to start the series of injections.'

The door flew open and Clint rushed inside. A tall, lanky man clad in dusty denims, he twisted his sweat-stained cowboy hat in his hands. 'How is he?'

'Not bad. Did you catch the dog?'

'Nope. Got away.' Karen gasped and Clint rubbed the back of his neck, revealing his own frustration. 'The neighbours and the entire sheriff's department are looking for him.'

'Did it appear rabid?' Andrew asked. 'Any signs of agitation or viciousness?'

Clint shook his head and Andrew persisted. 'What about any signs of paralysis, limping—that sort of thing?'

'He looked more scared than anything,' Clint said. 'I left some food and water for him while I was waiting for the sheriff to arrive and the dog ate like he was starved. He's shy of people, though. Took off like a bolt of lightning the minute I opened the gate.'

'We need the animal,' Andrew said. 'I'm sure you're right about the dog being domesticated, but we can't risk Travis's life on a guess.'

A distinct glimmer appeared in Karen's eyes and she blinked rapidly.

'You're right, we can't. I've heard...' Her lower lip quivered. 'I've heard those injections are awful.'

'They aren't pleasant, but technology has improved them significantly,' Andrew reassured her. 'The immunization consists of five injections, rather than the twenty required some years ago. We also administer the vaccine in the upper arm or thigh rather than in the abdominal area.

'First, he'll receive a dose of rabies immune globulin—the passive immunization—one-half injected around the bite itself and the remainder given intramuscularly. Then he'll receive the active immunizations today and again on days three, seven, fourteen and twenty-eight.

'If we find the dog in the meantime,' he continued, 'and its vaccinations are current, then we'll stop.'

Karen blew her nose, her eyes red-rimmed. Clint rubbed his son's back. 'What...?' He cleared his throat. 'What are his chances?'

'Of developing rabies?' At Clint's nod, Andrew recalled statistics. 'If an infected animal bites a person's leg he runs a ten per cent chance of developing rabies. A bite on the face, however, runs at about sixty per cent. As you can see, the odds are in Travis's favour.'

'Will you start the injections now?'

Andrew hesitated. 'We'll wait a few hours. Maybe Sheriff Swanson or his deputies will find the animal. It would certainly make life easier if they did.'

Karen cleared her throat. 'I washed the area with soap and water immediately, then brought him in. Will he need stitches?'

Andrew was glad to hear that Karen was focusing on

the most immediate problem, rather than dwelling on the what-ifs. 'Actually, we try to avoid suturing the wound whenever possible. That way it can drain and we prevent an abscess from forming. We're also not in any rush to stop the bleeding since the flow also helps to clean the wound. Unless, of course, he's bleeding profusely, which he isn't.'

Drew located a bottle of sterile water and a basin, then tugged on a pair of latex gloves. 'I want you to hop on the bed, Travis.' Aided by his father, Travis did as instructed.

'Now, lay your leg across this pan so I can rinse out the bite again.'

Travis's brown eyes stared at Drew soulfully. 'Is it gonna hurt?'

'No. As soon as I'm finished I'll tape on a bandage.'

'OK.'

While the parents looked on, Andrew performed his task. Once finished, he stripped off the gloves to wash his hands and pat Travis on the head. 'I'll call the sheriff and see what's the latest word.'

He returned a few minutes later, disheartened by the news he had to impart. 'They're still searching.' Glancing at his friends, he noted their tired features, their slumped shoulders.

'Go home,' Andrew ordered. 'I'll call you later.' The possibility of bringing Travis back for treatment went unspoken.

The day, which had started out with such promise, was now filled with a host of unexpected complications.

Andrew Prescott had to be the most infuriating man Mariah had ever met. She hated losing control. More importantly, she hated her weak spot to be revealed. Regardless, she intended to discover why he held her responsible and in such contempt for Kelly Evers leaving. She might have stepped onto a battleground by accident but she didn't intend to remain weaponless for long.

Mariah arrived at her final destination a few minutes later. There, she greeted an austere woman with short, straight, salt-and-pepper hair, and hoped the chill emanating from the lady resulted from overwork and not animosity. 'Hello.'

'Can I help you?' the woman asked, without a change in her grim countenance.

'I'm Mariah Henning. I'm the temporary med tech.'

'*Finally*, we see some help,' the woman declared in a brusque manner. 'It's about time, too. Nancy is dead on her feet.'

'I'm sorry to hear that. Is she inside?' Mariah tipped her head in the direction of the testing area.

'No, she's on East—the east wing. Should be back any minute. Have a seat.'

Mariah glanced at the woman's name-tag. 'Do you mind if I look around, Polly?'

'Suit yourself.'

Mariah strode past the clerk, noticing a tiny office before she entered the adjoining room which was filled with testing equipment.

Her gaze touched on a variety of instruments on the countertops. While the majority weren't the latest models, they also weren't as old as she had originally feared. She sauntered around the work area, feeling at ease. Having used these manufacturers' products before, it wouldn't take much training to relearn their operating essentials. Everything also appeared well cared-for, which added to her delight. The as-yet-unknown Nancy obviously subscribed to Mariah's own philosophy that instruments functioned better and lasted longer if properly maintained.

Racks of blood samples and test tubes were scattered at various locations on the countertops, along with a few opened test kits and reagents. Obviously Nancy had been called away while in the middle of her procedures. Even so, there was a method to the disarray.

In the background the latest Michael Bolton song ended and a radio announcer gave the call letters of his station, as a curly-headed brunette in her early to mid-twenties walked in and plonked her plastic carryall onto the nearest counter.

'Hi,' she said, sounding cheerful in spite of the shadows under her eyes. 'So you're my reinforcement. I'm Nancy Lathrop.'

'Mariah Henning. I'll be your assistant for the next six months or so, depending on when you hire someone.'

'Great.' Nancy ambled closer to Mariah and the semi-automated haematology analyzer, then slipped a face shield over her head. 'Hope you don't mind if we talk while I work,' she said, pulling on a fresh pair of gloves.

'Not at all.'

Nancy reached for a lavender-stoppered tube on her tray, inverted it several times then popped off the rubber cap so the instrument could aspirate the specimen. Next she made a blood smear. While it was drying she dipped a reagent strip into a urine sample. By the time the CBC results printed, the urinalysis was completed and the slide ready for staining.

'You're organized,' Mariah commented, secretly pleased. She and Nancy would work well together.

'I've had to be,' Nancy admitted, 'otherwise I'd never leave this place. Unfortunately, I hate the paperwork—ordering supplies, that sort of thing. Polly keeps the patient records and billing up to date, but the administrative side is in a mess. By any chance, you wouldn't be willing to muddle through all that, would you?'

The pleading expression on Nancy's face made Mariah laugh. 'I'd be happy to. I'm an old hand at shuffling paper. It comes from my days as supervisor.'

'I don't have such lofty aspirations. I'm happy to take care of the patients. The other stuff gives me a headache so the job is yours and with my blessing,' Nancy said fervently.

'Only until the next person comes along. I'm only temporary, remember?'

'Don't remind me,' Nancy said. 'Besides, I can always hope.'

Mariah guided her onto what she considered a more important subject. 'Tell me about your schedule. What time do I need to be here every morning, how do we divide up the load—that sort of thing?'

'Kelly and I rotated. One week I'd look after haematology, coag, urinalysis and blood bank, while she took care of chemistry and our reference lab work. If one of us was busier than the other we'd work together.'

'Good idea.'

'I start at six a.m. so I have the samples collected no later than seven. Then I run the tests specified as early a.m.—mostly glucoses, H and Hs, coagulation tests—so the nurses have the results before the doctors make their rounds at eight. I spend the rest of the day running the routine tests and whatever else happens to be ordered.

'When Kelly was here,' Nancy continued, 'we took turns coming at six and at eight. One would leave at three and the other would cover the lab until five.'

'And what do you do now?'

Nancy smiled as she placed a red-stoppered

Vacutainer tube into the centrifuge and turned the power knob. A soft whir grew louder as the motor picked up speed. 'I come at six and stay until four. I tried leaving earlier but whenever I did someone always called me back. The doctors usually co-operate and don't order lab work after five unless it's a real emergency.' She grinned. 'They do what they can to help.'

Wryly, Mariah wondered if Dr Prescott would extend her the same courtesy.

'Have you met Dr Prescott?' Nancy asked.

'Yes.' Under the circumstances, Mariah thought the less said the better.

'Isn't he wonderful? He's been so supportive. I don't know what I'd have done without him.' Without pausing for breath, she asked, 'When can you start?'

'Right away. Provided you can loan me a lab coat. When I arrived for my meeting with Gary Wright I wasn't prepared for a long stay.' The clothing in her suitcase fitted into one of two categories—suitable for business meetings or for relaxing at motels.

'One freshly shed lab coat coming up,' Nancy said.

'I can make do with the clothes I brought for a while,' Mariah said. 'However, in the near future, I'd like to drive home, pick up a few more things, and deal with the personal business I've let slide during the last few weeks.'

'Why not go tomorrow?'

Although the idea was music to her ears, Mariah declined. 'Dr Prescott wanted me to start immediately. I'd better stick to the time frame he wants.'

Nancy continued as if she hadn't spoken. 'Today's Monday. If you're back by, say, Wednesday or Thursday that's soon enough for me.'

'Thanks, but I don't think it would work. I don't want

to jeopardize my position here, especially since Dr Prescott made it quite plain in Gary Wright's office that he considers TLC and its employees as lower forms of life.'

Nancy waved aside her objection. 'Nonsense. I'll take care of it. Although I'd have thought he'd gotten over his animosity by now.'

Mariah's pulse speeded. She hadn't expected to find the answers to her questions concerning Andrew's attitude so easily. 'I know Kelly joined us a year ago,' she began, testing Nancy's reaction, 'yet Dr Prescott seems to be taking her defection personally.'

'It's understandable, I suppose.'

Before Mariah could ask why, Nancy cocked her head to something the radio announcer said then moved to turn up the volume. A deep voice came across the air waves.

'Anyone having any information on a dog meeting this description should contact the Niobrara County Sheriff's Department. This animal is considered a potential rabies threat. It's imperative that this dog be taken into custody as it could prevent a child from undergoing rabies vaccinations. To repeat, people in the Gallup area should be on the alert for a collie.'

'Hmm,' Nancy said, lowering the volume. 'I hope someone finds it.'

'I hope so, too.' Mariah directed the conversation back to their original topic. 'Why is it understandable for Dr Prescott to be upset over Kelly's leaving?'

Nancy shrugged. 'They were going to be married.'

Married? She performed a quick calculation in her head. Was Andrew the father of Kelly's baby?

The idea sent a sharp stab of pain through her chest. She didn't want it to be true but, after experiencing his charm, she understood how easily a woman could welcome him into her bed. Some would consider landing an attractive physician a veritable coup. On the other hand, why would anyone desert such a man, even under those circumstances?

She took a moment to compose herself. Weighing her words and adding just enough surprise to her voice, she asked, 'Really? Then why did she leave?'

'She wanted some excitement in her life, I guess. Although how she could give up a man like Andrew, or even want to, I'll never know.' Nancy shook her head, obviously puzzled by Kelly's decision.

'Have you kept in touch?' She waited for the answer with baited breath.

'No. As far as I can tell, she cut off all contact.'

Mariah swallowed hard. No wonder Andrew's animosity toward her ran so deep. Kelly had obviously severed all ties with friends and family to hide her out-of-wedlock pregnancy. It seemed extreme in this day and age, but the girl apparently had had her reasons.

If Kelly had gone to such drastic measures to keep her secret, Mariah couldn't in good conscience divulge the information without Kelly's permission. Andrew's low opinion of TLC Inc—and her—would have to stand unchallenged. Although Mariah ached to vindicate herself, she couldn't.

She tried not to dwell on why it mattered.

It was nearly six o'clock before Mariah parked her car in the driveway of 118 Clark Street. The day had been long and filled with surprises, but it had ended on a good note. With Mariah's help, Nancy had completed the pending lab work in record time. For the remainder of the afternoon Nancy had given Mariah a crash course on the chemistry analyzer's operation.

Now, with the key Gary Wright had given her, Mariah intended to check out her home for the next six months. Although the house came furnished, she intended to supplement its basic offerings with things from her own condo. Her grinder and fresh coffee beans were placed high on her list.

The warm air brought with it a sense of lethargy. For a few minutes she sat, staring at the building before her. The white frame house was small and compact, with dark blue shutters on its old-style eight-foot-high windows. It reminded her of her grandmother's home, right down to the front porch with a bench swing hanging from the rafters.

The smell of freshly cut grass from the neighbour's yard drifted in her direction. She hoped Gary had provided a mower; she didn't mind the work. The lawn was postage-stamp-sized so it wouldn't take her long—not like the three acres surrounding her childhood home. Then again, her father owned a riding rather than a push-type mower and the ability to drive made the task seem like fun rather than a chore.

She smiled. She and her sisters had spent many an hour arguing over whose turn it was, at least until her mother posted a schedule. Her parents had laughed about having the best manicured yard in the entire state of Kansas since the grass barely had time to grow before one of them was cutting it again.

Heaving a sigh, she slid out of the car and strode towards the porch steps. A turn of the key later she was inside. The interior had a closed-in smell, as if it had been vacant for some time. Even so, the furniture lacked any noticeable dust. Gary hadn't stretched the truth by mentioning it was nothing fancy, she thought. The living room boasted a sofa, one recliner, a coffee-table, desk and a lone seascape on the wall.

After perusing the sixties-decor kitchen, the two small bedrooms, complete with linen, and a bathroom with an old-fashioned claw-footed bathtub, she kicked off her heels and removed her pantihose. Padding outside barefooted, she sank onto the swing. It moved back and forth smoothly and squeaked only an occasional protest. Intending to enjoy it to the full, she added a can of lubricant to her list.

The peaceful evening and the gentle sway of the swing provided the balm she needed after her stressful day. The quiet air, broken only by the sound of children's laughter, bird calls and an occasional car engine, reminded her of the same ambience of her childhood environment.

Dave wouldn't have liked this place, she thought objectively. He'd been too much in tune with the fast pace of Denver to enjoy a slower lifestyle for long. She twisted the ring on her finger, staring at the rubies surrounding the diamond. Her job at TLC Inc, taken shortly after his death, had helped her deal with the unfulfilled plans they'd made. It was probably time to put the ring away, but she wasn't ready to relinquish it yet.

Forcing aside her maudlin feelings, which also seemed stronger when she was tired, she studied the neighbourhood. Two homes across the street had been recently built, their contemporary style contrasting with the old but well-kept houses on her side of the block. The house directly facing her was a red-bricked ranch-style dwelling with a struggling new lawn. Holes had been dug at precise intervals in obvious preparation for installing a fence.

The house next door was similar to hers in appearance with one exception. Hundreds of yellow daffodils surrounded the foundation and hundreds more covered the back yard. Struck by the cheerful and awe-inspiring sight, she hoped to meet the person responsible.

Her stomach rumbled, gearing her into action. She retrieved her shoes in order to bring her suitcases into the house.

After removing her garment bag, a box and two small cases, she was down to the last and also the largest. She bent over the back of the trunk to grab the case's handle, hoping her skirt hadn't crept up to indecent heights.

Suddenly a voice came from behind. 'Need any help?'

She whirled to face the owner of the voice, shocked to see he was Andrew Prescott.

CHAPTER THREE

'SORRY to scare you, but I thought you heard me coming.'

Mariah held a shaky hand to her racing heart. 'No, I didn't.' Deep in her thoughts, she doubted if she would have heard an army tank roll down the street.

'May I lend you a hand?'

'Um, sure,' she mumbled, wary of the situation and trying to second-guess his motives.

Andrew brushed her aside and grabbed the suitcase with both hands. Lifting it with ease, he set it on the concrete. Immediately she extended the handle so it could be rolled rather than carried.

He took hold of the bar. 'I'll take it.'

'I can manage.'

'I'm sure you can, but I insist.'

With a shrug, she picked up the garment bag, noticing he'd also commandeered one of the small suitcases. She led the way inside, amazed at his reverse transformation into the charismatic man she'd seen at the Winding Trails Inn.

'Where do you want these?' he asked.

She placed her burden next to the couch. 'In the bedroom.'

He disappeared in the direction she'd indicated while she took advantage of his momentary absence to retrieve the items left in the driveway. As she navigated the concrete stairs he opened the screen door, then took the bulky box out of her arms.

'Be careful,' Mariah cautioned. 'That's my photography equipment.'

He set the carton on the sofa table. 'Nice hobby.'

'Yes.' Calling her second love a mere hobby seemed trite. At one time it had been an important part of her life. She and Dave had spent many happy hours trekking through parks, the foothills and mountains in search of the perfect scene. To her regret, her desire to snap the shutter had died with him.

In recent months she'd occasionally come across something unusual which had sired a notion to begin again. Although she'd started carrying her camera, she hadn't been able to take that final step of taking photos on her own. She wasn't ready to sever another link with her fiancé.

She changed the subject to avoid a lengthy explanation. 'I'd offer you a drink, but all I have is water.'

'That's OK because I came to ask you to dinner.'

Her jaw went slack. 'You did?'

'Yes. As my way of apologizing.'

'I see.' She took a moment to study him through narrowed eyes. 'Are you positive you don't have a twin?'

His unexpected grin was wide and revealed a silver-crowned premolar. 'Sorry. What you see is what you get.'

'No offence, but I've seen you twice today and I've encountered a different Andrew Prescott each time.' She folded her arms. 'To be honest, I'm not sure which one is standing in front of me.'

'Probably a combination,' he admitted. 'If it will make you feel better, I promise to be on my best behaviour.'

Suspiciously she asked, 'Then you've changed your opinion of TLC?' And me? she wanted to add, but didn't.

'I'm willing to be open-minded.'

Although it wasn't the answer she'd hoped for, at least it was a start in the right direction. 'I accept your apology. Are you sure you want to eat with the so-called enemy?'

His mouth twitched into a faint smile. 'Planning on poisoning my drink?'

Her face warmed under his teasing tone. 'I was about to accuse you of the same thing,' she said lightly.

'Since we've exposed that plot, we'll both be safe. So, how about dinner?'

Mariah made an instant decision. If he could act graciously then she couldn't do any less. 'Why not?' She blurted out her next thought. 'Where are we going?'

'The Pioneer Grill. It's a bar on the edge of town.' He glanced at his watch. 'It's late so we'll avoid most of the supper crowd.'

'Can I have fifteen minutes to change?'

His perusing glance sent a tingle along her spine and all the way down to her toes. 'Sure. I want to check on the progress of my carpet-layer—I live across the street by the way—so come out when you're ready.'

Across the street? she thought, unsure if she should be dismayed or elated. She swallowed hard. 'I'll hurry.'

Rushing into the bedroom to strip off her wrinkled skirt and white sleeveless top, she considered this new piece of information. Although Andrew seemed to be offering an olive branch she wondered if he had an ulterior motive. Considering his animosity towards her company in general and herself in particular for recruiting Kelly Evers, perhaps he was only on a fact-finding mission to discredit her and her agency.

Don't overreact, she told herself as she tugged on her last pair of clean jeans and pulled a V-necked yellow and white striped cotton T-shirt over her head. You've been reading too many espionage novels with complicated plot twists, betrayals and hidden agendas. She was Mariah Henning in Gallup, Wyoming—a tiny dot on the map—not James Bond in Budapest, Washington or London.

Without any evidence to the contrary, she'd believe that his motives were pure, that he was offering her a taste of western hospitality. As for her misgivings, she'd steer the conversation away from controversial subjects like Kelly Evers.

She slipped on a pair of sandals, tucked a loose strand of hair back into her braid and freshened her make-up. After glancing at her reflection in the tiny bathroom mirror, she pronounced herself ready.

Ready for what she wasn't sure.

The last time she'd gone out with a man the evening had been an unmitigated disaster. She'd agreed to the invitation, both as a favour to her friend, Barbara, and to test the dating waters again. Unfortunately, she'd only intended to dip her toes in the pool while her date had expected a dive off the deep end. In his opinion, her nomadic lifestyle included having a man in every port and he intended to be the one in that particular town. Since then she'd kept Dave's ring firmly in place on her finger, telling the truth to only a few, carefully screened individuals to avoid repeat incidents.

The knot of tension in her stomach slowly dissolved. Although Andrew knew the facts, he didn't seem the type to harbour such expectations or to take advantage of a situation. Also, his resentment was too deeply entrenched to be uprooted over a single meal, no matter how congenial the atmosphere. In any event, she hoped to find his flaw, to discover the reason behind Kelly's flight. Without the critical information her immunity to his masculine allure would fail.

A minute later Mariah met Andrew on the sidewalk. He, too, had changed into a more informal outfit, consisting of blue jeans, a tan long-sleeved western-style shirt, brown cowboy boots and a chocolate-brown stetson.

If what she saw was what she got, he looked more like a cowboy out for a night on the town rather than a doctor who held life and death in his hands. Regardless of the incongruity, his casual attire suited him as well as his professional clothes.

'Hope you're hungry,' he said, escorting her to his Land Cruiser. 'They have good food and plenty of it.'

'I am.'

Ten minutes later he turned into the Pioneer Grill's parking lot, sending up a shower of gravel as the tyres crunched the pebbles.

The building itself appeared weatherbeaten and worn. Although the exterior could have been carefully crafted to achieve its appearance of antiquity, a few loose shingles and a sagging section of guttering suggested otherwise.

A small, narrow building stood about fifty feet from the restaurant, a half-moon carved in the door. 'I assume this establishment has indoor plumbing,' Mariah commented.

Andrew laughed. 'The outhouse is purely for ambience.'

'What a relief.'

'According to Chester Jakes, it was in working order before he moved it here as a conversation piece. It's a two-seater and comes with its own catalogue for your convenience.' He grinned.

She returned his smile. 'I'll take you at your word.'

The decor inside the restaurant was as rustic as its exterior. A bar ran along the length of one side of the huge room and signs, advertising various brands of beer, lit the walls.

Intimate booths lined the opposite side and tables filled the space in between. Every chair was occupied, testimony to customer satisfaction with the cuisine. The odour of grilled meat and onions tantalized her taste buds and her stomach rumbled once again. Luckily, the murmur of people talking, an occasional guffaw, the chink of silverware on plates and ice in glasses covered the sound.

A couple vacated their booth and Andrew steered her toward their spot before the table had been cleared.

'Have to move quickly in here or you won't eat,' he said, sliding onto the padded vinyl bench across from her.

A jeans-clad brunette waitress in her forties appeared to remove the dishes. 'What'll you have, Drew?'

'Your evening special. Sirloin, medium–well with fried onions on the side. Baked potato, Blue cheese dressing. Oh, and ice tea.'

Balancing the plates, cups and silverware, the woman glanced at Mariah. 'What about you?'

It sounded delicious. 'The same.'

Mariah eyed the fresh ashtray the waitress had left on the clean table. 'Looks like the concept of no smoking in public places hasn't caught on here.'

'Afraid not. People in Gallup aren't receptive to change. Most folks are too set in their ways to care about being politically correct.'

Mariah glanced around the room. 'I gathered that.'

Under the table, her knees brushed against his. The

contact was accidental, and yet seemed so intimate. For a fleeting moment she wished he'd sat beside her rather than across from her, then mentally chided herself for entertaining such thoughts. Even though he was polite and attentive at the moment, a few hours ago she'd been lower than pond scum in his opinion.

'Nancy tells me you're leaving tomorrow.'

She tipped her chin to gaze into his eyes, daring him to make a comment. 'If I'm to stay for six months I need a few more things than what I brought with me.'

He remained silent and she added, 'I cleared it with Gary. I'll be back on Thursday.'

'OK.'

'What? No argument?' Although she spoke in a bantering tone, she was serious.

Andrew shook his head. 'I should have realized you wouldn't be prepared to stay since you handle more of the administrative duties.'

How did he know that? Or had he simply guessed correctly? 'You seem familiar with my job description.'

He lifted one shoulder in a shrug. 'After Kelly met you at a job fair in Scottsbluff she couldn't say enough good things about you. I've known her a long time and I can't remember anyone impressing her as much as you did.'

Mariah's face warmed under his comment and she felt a stirring of unease. She broke eye contact and drew circles in the condensation on her glass. 'I don't recall doing or saying anything that would warrant her to feel that way. We talked about a variety of subjects.'

'According to her, you were passionate about your job. She was envious of the people you'd met, the places you'd been, the things you'd done.'

'I spoke from my experience,' she said stiffly. 'I stated

facts, I didn't glamorize my travels at all. However, I've seen a number of interesting places and met many interesting people. I wouldn't have enjoyed those opportunities if I'd kept my position at National Jewish.'

'After living life in the proverbial fast lane, can you handle staying in Gallup? Working for five physicians in a thirty-bed hospital?'

She'd asked herself the same question but kept the knowledge to herself. 'I grew up on a farm in western Kansas, not too far from a town about this size. I can shift gears to a slower pace for six months.' At least she hoped so.

'You won't get bored?'

'Boredom affects everyone at some point in time,' she pointed out. 'Living in a large city doesn't make one immune.'

He took a large swallow of his tea. 'We're trying to increase our bed capacity, but we're having a difficult time.'

'Government regulations?' she guessed.

'No. Staffing. We aren't exactly the hub of Wyoming. When we lose a trained professional it hurts the whole community.'

Mariah narrowed her eyes. 'Are you suggesting—?'

'I'm not suggesting anything other than to consider those facts when you're recruiting in small areas.'

She leaned her elbows on the table. 'I'm very much aware of your dilemma. Most of our business comes from small hospitals such as yours.'

His eyes widened slightly and a small smile crossed her mouth. 'We don't steal our staff from the rural areas so the metropolitan health care system can flourish.'

'TLC is based in Denver,' he pointed out. 'Also, Kelly

is working in Sheridan. I wouldn't classify it as a small town.'

'Our company headquarters are in Denver because it provided us with a large base from which to draw our initial workforce. As for Kelly, she's establishing a lab in a new physician's clinic and will work there until the manager can hire someone permanent. When a facility requests TLC we go.'

A slow grin appeared on his face. '"TLC To Go." Catchy phrase.'

The tense moment had apparently passed. 'I'll turn in your idea the next time we update our corporate image.'

He leaned back in a relaxed pose. 'Besides photography, what do you do in your spare time?'

Relieved by the change in topic, she laughed. 'My job doesn't allow for much spare time. If I have an evening free, I'm usually too exhausted to tackle anything physical. When I worked at the hospital with Dave, my fiancé, we'd spend hours searching for camera spots. At other times we played tennis, visited museums, attended concerts, browsed in libraries.' Remembering those happy occasions, she fell silent.

'How long has it been?' His voice was soft and touched her like a caress.

'A little over two years.'

He looked thoughtful. 'Before you joined TLC.'

'Yes.' She cleared her throat. 'Dave was a chemist on my shift so we started out as colleagues, then friends. Afterwards...' her voice quivered '...there were too many reminders everywhere I went.'

'So you changed the scenery.'

She nodded. 'I'd considered selling my condominium but I couldn't.' Her home had been her haven until Dave's death, and now it wasn't. Although they hadn't lived together because she was old-fashioned enough to reject the idea, the rooms were filled with memories—memories of happy times and plans for the future.

Andrew's gaze was sympathetic. 'What happened?'

She sipped her tea. 'While he was in surgery for a hernia repair he went into cardiac arrest. They weren't able to revive him.'

He leaned across the table to cover her hand with his. 'I'm sorry.'

'Yes, well, tell me about yourself,' she said, changing the subject once again.

'I grew up at Redbird, which is about twenty miles east of here. My grandparents lived on a small ranch outside of Gallup and I inherited it after they passed away. Since I couldn't maintain it properly and keep my practice going at the same time I rented the property to some friends of mine. The Spauldings.'

He drew a deep breath. 'Unfortunately, a stray dog bit young Travis this afternoon.'

'I heard about it on the radio. Have they found the animal yet?'

'No. I'm afraid we'll have to start the rabies vaccinations. Fortunately, the vaccine has been improved, but even so it won't be a pleasant experience.'

'I don't imagine so.'

'By the way, what did you think of our lab?'

'I'm impressed, actually. I've been in a lot worse situations. Your equipment seems fairly up to date and well maintained.' Mariah refrained from commenting on the lab's out-of-the-way location. He might construe her observation as finding fault or lodging a complaint and she didn't want to ruin their pleasant evening.

'It is awkward being so far away from the rest of the hospital,' he said.

Mariah blinked as she stared at his face. How had he known her very thought?

He grinned. 'Don't look so surprised. You aren't the first person who's commented on the poor location.'

'Are you trying to correct the situation or—?'

The moment was lost as the waitress interrupted with their plates of food. The aroma from the steak in front of her made Mariah's mouth water and she expectantly took her first bite.

It was like sheer ambrosia. She closed her eyes as she savoured the taste. 'It's delicious.'

'I'm glad you think so,' he said with amusement.

Throughout the meal Andrew regaled her with tales of local folklore, interspersed with stories from his medical school days. By the time Mariah had eaten her fill, half of her steak and potato remained.

'I hate to waste this, but I can't swallow another bite,' she said.

'Take it home,' he advised. 'It'll keep in the fridge.'

Ten minutes later they left the smoke-filled room with Mariah carrying a styrofoam container. The sun had descended to an angle that caused it to shine directly into her face. She shielded her eyes as she walked toward Andrew's Land Cruiser, conscious of his hand hovering at the back of her waist.

The gesture was a courtesy, nothing more, she reminded herself. Unfortunately, her nerve endings didn't consider it as such. They felt as if she were on fire— warm, then hot. Even a reminder that he was spoken for didn't quench the flames.

While he opened the passenger door for her she glanced toward the outhouse. A small out-of-place shadow clung to the side of the building, and she paused.

'Ready?' he asked.

'Wait a minute. I thought I saw something odd over there...' The shadow disappeared and she shook her head. 'I must have been mistaken.'

He scanned the area. 'What was it?'

Her first thought had been a coyote or a fox, but those animals tended to stay away from populated areas. Since he might fault her with an overactive imagination she shrugged off her observation as unimportant. 'I'm not sure. It was probably someone's dog.' She glanced away, ready to climb into the vehicle, but out of the corner of one eye she saw movement.

Mariah refocused her gaze. This time an animal stepped out of the shadows. 'I was right. It's only a dog. Looks like a collie.'

She'd no sooner spoken the words than realization dawned. 'Is it possible—?'

Andrew met her gaze, his face mirroring her own thoughts. The next instant she rushed around the front of the vehicle for a closer inspection.

A firm hand on her arm prevented her advance. 'Don't go any closer,' he ordered.

'I was just trying to see it,' she defended herself. 'He's just standing there. It *is* a collie. Poor thing. He looks half-starved. Do you suppose it's the same one—?'

'Don't go any closer,' he ordered again. 'I'm calling the sheriff. Keep an eye on him. If he leaves we'll need to know the direction he's headed.'

Andrew opened the driver's door and reached for his cell phone. While he punched numbers Mariah stared at the collie. Although she'd never seen a rabid animal, she'd heard many stories about foaming at the mouth, twitching and aggressive behaviour or, in some cases, lethargy—none of which described the creature before her. The dog seemed to be waiting patiently for someone or something. Considering that this was a restaurant, perhaps someone routinely left table scraps out of pity.

The container in her hand gave her an idea. She inched her way forward, then placed the open box on the ground at a point halfway between Andrew's vehicle and the dog. She retreated quickly, mentally justifying her actions. Perhaps the animal would stay long enough to eat, giving someone from the humane society enough time to arrive.

The dog raised its head, as if catching the scent of food. It hesitated, then advanced a step as if its stomach had overridden its survival instincts. Guided by her intuition and farming experience, Mariah didn't move. If the collie perceived the slightest threat it would bolt. Watching Mariah with a wary eye, the collie hurried to its supper and wolfed it down.

Andrew came from behind and placed one hand on her shoulder. 'What did you do?'

His breath whispered softly against her neck, sending a shiver down her spine. 'I gave him my leftovers. I thought he might be more apt to stay. This sounds crazy, but he reminds me of Lassie. I loved that show when I was a kid.'

'Yeah, well, the real Lassie didn't bite people,' he said in a dry tone. 'The sheriff and one of our vets are on the way.'

Gradually a few other people joined them. To Mariah's disappointment, the collie bounded away, leaving the container licked clean. Just as she thought the dog would disappear over the horizon it stopped near the outhouse and waited.

'I'll get my gun,' someone said.

Mariah's reply was quick and forceful as she pivoted

to face the speaker. 'No. It doesn't have rabies. I'm sure of it.'

'You're not a veterinarian,' Andrew reminded her. 'Even if you were, you can't make that diagnosis from this distance.' He nodded to the youthful cowboy, who hurried toward a Chevrolet pickup truck at the far end of the lot.

Mariah watched the man remove a rifle from the gun rack over the cab's rear window. 'Can't we at least wait for the sheriff? He might be able to catch him without...' She swallowed hard. 'Without...'

'Killing him?' he finished. 'I doubt it. You've grown up in the country. What do you think happens to stray or wild animals if they bite someone?'

She knew the exact procedure. The animal was euthanized and its brain sent to the state laboratory for examination. If the technicians found Negri bodies in the tissue, the diagnosis was certain; the animal had rabies.

'But what if the dog is someone's lost pet? What if its vaccinations are current?'

'And what if they aren't?' he countered. 'I'm not anxious to kill the collie because I like animals too, but, given the choice between saving a dog and saving a child, there's no contest.'

She sighed. 'I know.' She glanced at the collie, who stared back at her with soulful eyes, and then at the cowboy who approached with his rifle. He looked about eighteen, too young in her opinion to have developed any skill. 'Are you a good shot?'

He appeared affronted. 'Lady, I've hunted practically all of my life. One bullet is all it'll take.'

'Make sure,' Mariah ordered. Unable to watch him take aim, she turned away. A hush descended until suddenly a sharp whistle broke the silence.

A portly man, wearing a white cook's apron liberally spattered with grease, rounded the corner of the restaurant with a plate in his hand.

'What's goin' on, folks?' he asked.

Mariah noticed that the dog's ears perked and his tail wagged before he let out a welcoming bark.

'Hey, Chester,' Andrew called out. 'We think the collie over there bit the Spaulding boy.'

Chester scratched his balding head. 'You don't say. I've been leaving food for him since he started coming around two weeks ago. Awful skittish. He won't let me get within arm's reach. Then, again, I haven't tried too hard either.'

The cowboy lowered his rifle. 'What do you want me to do, Doc?'

Mariah had an idea. 'Find a leash.'

The three men stared at her as if she'd sprouted wings. 'I'll try my luck,' she said.

'I think not,' Andrew retorted. 'I refuse to risk it.'

'I'm taking the risk, not you.'

'Sorry, but if you think I'll allow you to endanger yourself you're mistaken.'

'This could be your only chance at catching him alive.'

'He's a stray,' Andrew said a trifle impatiently. 'Without an owner, he'll be put down at the end of the ten-day period anyway.' He held up his hands to forestall her arguments. 'I didn't say it was right or that I'm in favour of it. I'm only stating protocol which, if you recall, is for public safety.'

Chester rubbed his bewhiskered face, as if pondering the situation. 'He's wearing a collar with a tag, but I can't get close enough to read it. Might be he *does* have an owner who'd want him back.'

Andrew focused his gaze on the older man. 'You're positive?'

'My eyesight ain't what it was, but I can sure tell a tag when I see one.'

'What if the owner doesn't want him? He wouldn't be the first animal to be dumped out in the middle of nowhere,' Andrew said.

Before Mariah could voice her claim Chester shrugged. 'Then I'll take him. I've been looking for a dog to replace my Matilda anyway.'

Although she was curious to know if Matilda had been his wife or a former pet, Mariah didn't ask. The main thing was that the collie would have a home. The tension in her shoulders diminished.

'I've got a length of clothesline inside. We can use that.' Chester hurried off to retrieve it.

'We'll wait for the vet,' Andrew stated in an unequivocal tone. 'He'll have a tranquillizer gun.'

'It won't do any good if the dog leaves before he arrives,' she pointed out.

'He won't. Not with him here.' Andrew motioned to the cowboy with the rifle.

'At least let me try,' she pleaded, eyeing the weapon with some distaste. Although she'd grown up in an area where hunting pheasant and other wildlife wasn't uncommon, and was often necessary to control the population, she had never liked the practice. 'If anything goes wrong, Buffalo Bill can do his thing.'

Once again Andrew shook his head. 'I won't risk you being injured.'

Mariah laid a hand on his arm. 'He's frightened, but he ate my supper. He knows my scent.'

'Frightened animals have strong survival instincts. I don't want to treat two patients for possible rabies.'

She grinned, hoping to add some levity. 'I don't want you to either, but I can do it. My family raises Australian shepherds so I know how to approach animals. At least give me a chance.'

A flock of crows rose above the elm trees in the distance. The dog glanced in their direction, then moved as if he intended to search for food elsewhere.

'We'll wait,' Andrew said in an unequivocal tone. He turned to the young cowboy to give him instructions. At the same time Chester returned, brandishing the white clothesline.

Before Andrew could stop her, Mariah rushed to the cook's side and grabbed the rope. After fashioning it into an impromptu leash, she set Chester's fresh plate of food next to the empty styrofoam container. This time she didn't leave, but crouched down to wait.

'Here, boy,' she crooned, ignoring Andrew's muttered imprecations coming from behind.

The collie cocked its head, considering this development, but hunger obviously overruled his reluctance. His first step was tentative, then grew more bold as he approached. Mariah remained still, murmuring words of encouragement. 'Come on, boy. We won't hurt you.'

Finally the dog stood within arm's reach and began to eat. Mariah inched her way closer, still speaking softly. Tears clogged her throat as she stared at what used to be a beautiful coat. Cockleburrs matted the shaggy fur and a swollen tick was attached behind one ear. A partially healed cut stretched across one paw and she could count his ribs. In the background, car tyres crunched on the gravel, but she ignored the newcomer. She couldn't afford to distract the collie.

He lifted his head, as if sensing her motive, and in a flash she slipped on the noose. The animal reared, its eyes wide with fright and its lips curled menacingly.

A shot rang out. The creature's leg gave way and he blinked in obvious surprise.

Oh, God, she thought, horrified. Her grip slackened at the same moment as the collie recovered. The line slipped through her fingers while the dog bounded away as fast as the dart in his shoulder muscle would allow.

'Here, boy!' she cried, hoping to coax him to return. As she'd suspected, her efforts were futile.

Furious, she faced the approaching group, recognizing Andrew, Chester, the young cowboy and the middle-aged sheriff from his khaki uniform and silver badge. Another man in his thirties, the one who carried a rifle in his hand, wore what seemed was the area's dress code—blue jeans—and a tan and blue striped shirt. An Atlanta Braves baseball cap, however, covered his head rather than the usual cowboy hat.

'What have you done?' she demanded. 'Why did you shoot him? He was scared. That's all. He wasn't attacking me.'

'Strictly a precaution,' the fellow drawled. 'Used a fast-acting tranquillizer so he shouldn't get far.'

'You could have hit me,' she railed, reacting to the possibility of wearing the dart herself.

'Not a chance,' he said, sounding cocky. 'I had a good bead on him. You weren't in any danger.'

'Gee, thanks. That makes me feel better.' She laced her words with sarcasm.

Andrew moved in closer. 'Mariah Henning, meet Bill Townsend. Our vet.'

Bill flashed her an easygoing grin. 'You have a nice touch with animals.'

'We'll never know. You shot him before I could calm him down.'

He shrugged, clearly undaunted by her outburst. 'He was too wrought up to give in without a fight. It will be easier to assess his condition if he's sedated.' He stared into the distance. 'Looks like he's down.'

The collie staggered a few more steps, then slumped to the ground. Mariah kept pace with the group to reach the animal's side.

Bill laid his weapon on the ground and knelt to examine the fallen collie. 'Pulse is good. He's wearing a tag but...' he leaned closer to peer at the metal circle '...the engraving is nearly worn off. Might take some time to track down his owner.'

'Let me know as soon as you do,' Andrew said. 'No matter what time of day or night.'

'Will do.' Bill stroked the animal's coat, gathered the dog to his chest then rose with ease. 'Feels like he's been on his own for some time. Not much weight to him.'

'Don't worry. I'll fatten him up,' Chester said.

Reading concern in Bill's gentle touch, Mariah regretted her earlier remarks. The man had acted to protect the dog and its handlers from further injury. 'I'm sorry for yelling at you,' she said, contrite.

Bill grinned. 'My wife gets high-strung when she's excited, too. I won't hold it against you.'

Unsure if she was being flattered or placated, she remained silent in the interest of peace.

While the sheriff, Chester and Bill made their way to a pickup with TOWNSEND VETERINARY CLINIC emblazoned on the door, Andrew grabbed Mariah's arms.

'Are you OK?'

'I'm fine.'

'No scratches?'

She wondered briefly at the worry in his voice, then disregarded it. 'No scratches.'

His sigh sounded like relief. Before she realized what was happening he'd gathered her to his chest.

'Of all the wilful, stubborn, *stupid* things to do... Don't ever do that again,' he ordered.

Hearing his tirade, she hid her smile against his shoulder. 'I had everything under control.'

He muttered something that sounded suspiciously like, 'Spare me from smart-aleck women.'

His steady heartbeat throbbed under her fingertips and his scent filled her nose with a heady mixture of hickory and other masculine fragrances. His arms were warm, his body solid, and she felt secure leaning against his frame. His mouth hovered over hers, and before she could protest his lips came upon hers in a bruising kiss. She hadn't realized until this very moment how much she missed this small intimacy, this feeling of being loved and cherished. Her arms snaked to his back. Every muscle, every sinew, seemed alive under her fingertips. She revelled under the mastery of his touch, giving of herself in return.

A car horn honked, breaking the mood and bringing her to earth with a thud.

Expecting to see Dave's familiar features—his light brown hair, which tended to be long, the scar beneath his left eye from an encounter with a baseball bat, his perpetual grin—she found Andrew's instead.

Her breath caught and she propelled herself out of his arms. What had she done?

Andrew stared at her, appearing equally stunned. 'Amazing.'

Gravel crunched and a cloud of dust rose. 'Everyone's leaving,' she said inanely, hugging her arms to halt the chill spreading through her. 'We should, too.'

She blinked to assuage the burning sensation behind her eyelids and avoided his gaze. Her reaction, as well as her memory lapse regarding her fiancé, distressed her beyond belief. The entire event had been a mistake generated by the relief of the moment, and was best forgotten, she told herself. His kiss, its intensity, didn't mean a thing.

In spite of her justifications, she felt odd and unsettled. She stole a glance at Andrew.

He opened his mouth, as if intending to comment, then closed it as if he'd changed his mind. Finally, he nodded. Perhaps he'd also recognized their moment of insanity and preferred not to analyze it. 'You're right. I'll take you home.'

As if sensing her attempt to distance herself from what had happened, he didn't touch her. She was both relieved and disappointed.

'Tired?' he asked.

'It's been a long day,' she admitted.

After a silent drive through Gallup's darkened streets, he parked in front of his house. She hopped out before he could open the door.

'I had a nice time,' she said politely. 'I hope everything works out with the Spauldings.'

'Me, too.' He hesitated. 'This isn't the best time to ask…'

'Go ahead,' she said, preoccupied with discovering a way to bolster her immunity to his toe-curling kiss.

The streetlight cast shadows across the serious lines of his face. He took a deep breath, then squared his shoulders. 'Would you release Kelly from her contract?'

CHAPTER FOUR

MARIAH stared at Andrew in disbelief. 'You want me to do what?'

'I'd like you to release Kelly from her current contract. Assign her to us.' He spoke in the same manner as a person spoke to a small child.

His audacity made her temper simmer. 'I can't.' She marched away.

He followed her across the street. 'Why not?'

'Because we have a legal obligation to the clinic in Sheridan,' she said, stating what she thought was obvious.

'Send someone else to take over for her.'

She exaggeratedly mimed tapping her forehead in thought. 'Correct me, but you *insisted* on specific terms for Gallup Memorial's contract—namely, that whoever was assigned to your facility would stay for the duration. Now you want to change the terms. Do you abide by your agreements only if the situation and the mood suit you?'

The muscle in his jaw tensed. 'No. I simply thought this arrangement would work out best for everyone.'

She folded her arms. 'It won't. I can't believe you're asking me to pull rank.'

'I'm not. I just thought you could send Kelly back here. Temporarily.'

'I don't need your help in scheduling my staff,' she ground out. 'Even if I wanted to assign Kelly here—and, mind you, I don't—I can't.' Her tone was flat. Although she refused to admit it, she felt rejected and used. 'It wouldn't be fair.'

'Temps could be released for a personal emergency,' he reminded her.

'Which usually deals with illness or a death. I won't juggle schedules or change our policies to suit your purposes. In any case, the employee has to initiate the request. I can't do it for them.' She narrowed her eyes. 'How would you feel if I tried to renege on the terms of Gallup's agreement?'

Before he could answer a painful thought seared her mind. 'You accused me of enticement, but you're just as guilty.'

He wrinkled his forehead until his eyebrows became a straight line. 'What are you talking about?'

'Dinner. Was your invitation a persuasive ruse so I'd comply with your request?' The idea that his earth-moving kiss might have been part of his attempt sent a flood of disappointment through her.

His 'no' was emphatic. 'To be honest, I didn't think of it until a few minutes ago.'

She unlocked her door. 'Oh, really.'

'It's true.'

The knob turned under her hand. 'I'm running a business, not a dating service. If you want to mend your relationship with Kelly you'll have to do it without me acting as intermediary.'

Before she could cross the threshold he forestalled her by gripping her elbow. 'This isn't about mending my relationship.'

She raised one eyebrow. 'It isn't?'

'We may have unfinished business between us,' he admitted, releasing his hold, 'but it isn't the reason behind my request. Her mother is a patient of mine. She has ITP—idiopathic thrombocytopenia—'

'I know what it is,' Mariah interrupted. 'Her platelet count is low due to an unknown cause.'

'Yes. In any event, Virginia Evers's health during the past six months has deteriorated. She needs her daughter.'

Her resolve wavered. 'Does Kelly know?'

'About the ITP?' At Mariah's nod, he said, 'We diagnosed her mother about eighteen months ago.'

She paused, allowing her brain to assimilate the information. 'Am I understanding you correctly? Kelly was aware of the situation before she left?'

'Yes.'

Mariah wanted to throw up her hands. 'Then I won't interfere. She made her decision.'

'Virginia's disease appears to be in remission, but her emotional state is precarious. Having Kelly nearby would boost her morale.'

She hated to sound so callous, but meddling in other people's affairs didn't appeal to her. 'I'm sorry to hear about Mrs Evers's condition, but you'll have to deal with Kelly yourself.'

His tone matched his stiff posture. 'Kelly doesn't believe me when I say her mother is depressed.'

'What about her father?'

'Winston's relationship with his daughter isn't the best. He's one of those opinionated men who's set in his ways. Compromise isn't part of his vocabulary.'

Probably the main reason behind Kelly's leaving, Mariah thought. The girl had obviously considered the job opportunity with TLC a godsend and had grabbed it with both hands. Yet it didn't explain why she chose to run from Andrew as well.

'And you think I can convince her to come back? Even temporarily?'

'She'll pay attention to you.'

Although sympathetic toward Mrs Evers, Mariah considered it inappropriate for her as Kelly's employer to step into the middle of a private matter.

'I can't help you.' She rubbed her forearms, feeling the absence of the sun's heat as it dropped closer to the western horizon. 'Sorry.' She turned to go inside.

Andrew grabbed her arm. 'Can't? Or won't?'

'Both. I can't meddle in my employee's problems and I don't force my people to work where they don't want to go.' She hated the way she sounded so heartless, but she didn't have any other choice. Kelly had burned her bridges a year ago. It wasn't up to Mariah to rebuild them.

'Don't you care that her family needs her?'

She did, but she shrugged, pretending nonchalance. 'It's unfortunate, but business is business.'

His eyes narrowed. 'So your blasted contracts are more important than people's needs? Good God, you're more hardhearted than I'd ever imagined.'

The scathing remark pierced her to the quick but she hid her dismay under an impassive exterior.

He dropped her arm as quickly as if it had turned into a sprig of poison ivy. 'Now I understand why Kelly was so enamoured with you. You're both the same. You're both running away from your responsibilities.'

'That's not true.'

He raised one eyebrow. 'Isn't it? I'm sorry to have bothered you, Ms Henning,' he said, his voice as stiff as his posture. 'I won't make the mistake of asking you to involve yourself with the people of this community again.'

Andrew marched down the steps, his heels clicking on the concrete as he made his way to his Land Cruiser. The door slammed with the intensity of a gunshot before he revved the engine and drove away.

Mariah sank onto the porch swing. How had a simple job become so complicated?

Why was Mariah making this so complicated? Andrew fumed as he stormed toward his vehicle. Why wouldn't she encourage Kelly to come home? He'd needed someone to talk some sense into her, more for Virginia's sake than his, and Mariah had seemed the obvious choice.

Just as he'd suspected, Ms Henning possessed a heart of stone. Unfortunately, being right gave him little comfort. For once he'd wanted to be wrong.

His cell phone rang. Frustrated by his defeat, he snapped a greeting.

'Drew, this is Bill. Hope I'm not calling at a bad time.'

'No.'

Bill chuckled. 'Struck out, huh? That explains the bad mood.'

Andrew bit back a retort. 'What do you want, Townsend?'

Bill's teasing tone turned serious. 'Thought you'd like to know about the collie. We haven't been able to track down the tag yet. Near as I can tell, the dog didn't come from these parts.'

'When will you know?'

'It's hard to say. I'll keep you posted.'

'Thanks.' Andrew broke the connection as he parked underneath the Winding Trails Inn's flashing red neon sign. He strode inside to retrieve the key, his boot heels thumping against the concrete in rapid staccato.

'Thought you'd show up before now,' Burt said in greeting as he removed a key from the pegboard hanging on the wall behind the counter. 'So the lady's stayin' in town for a while.'

'That's the arrangement,' Andrew said, keeping his voice noncommittal.

'Think you can get her to stay longer? Maybe even permanent-like?'

'No. She's staying six months. No more, no less.' And if she thought she could wiggle out of her contract when she was intent on holding Kelly to hers she could think again. Andrew headed for the door before Burt could ask any more questions. Mariah Henning was one subject he didn't want to discuss *or* think about.

Yet, as he walked into room ten a few minutes later, he found it an impossible task. The room was neat, but a light fragrance—a cross between a floral scent and a fruity one—remained. He recognized it immediately as Mariah's.

Thankful that she didn't lean toward something cloying, he sank onto the bed to pull off his boots, then stretched out on top of the wedding-ring-patterned quilt to click on the television. The scent seemed stronger, as if she'd slept on the very pillow tucked under his head.

His imagination ran riot before he could stop himself. He pictured her with her hair spread across the pillows, her eyes closed, a dreamy smile on her face. Her virginal white nightgown dipped off one shoulder, revealing a creamy expanse of skin that begged to be caressed. In sleep, the hem of her gown had ridden upwards to expose the long shapely legs he'd seen covered in a ragged pair of denim shorts.

Sheer determination brought his body back to a relaxed state. Her kiss had been as powerful as rocket fuel, but he didn't want to feel an attraction for a woman so clearly unconcerned about others. And yet how could a woman who responded with such passion fall into that category?

The woman he'd intended to spend the rest of his life with had never melted in his arms the way Mariah had. The simple observation underscored what he'd come to accept over the past six months—basing a marriage solely on friendship was a huge mistake.

He and Kelly had been buddies since he was an eight-year-old, spending his first summer with his grandparents, and they'd shared their innermost thoughts. They'd drifted apart during college but once he'd returned to establish his practice in Gallup they'd spent hours in each other's company once again.

Her love for the family farm, her nesting instincts, her hopes to expand the scope of medical care in Gallup, had dovetailed with his own. Naturally, his thoughts had turned toward marriage. With his biological clock ticking, he'd proposed.

She'd gently refused, begging for time. After a sudden trip to Nebraska she'd announced her desire for a more exciting life. Her uncharacteristic actions had puzzled him until he'd learned of her meeting with TLC Inc. Someone had influenced Kelly and he'd blamed Mariah Henning.

Hindsight, however, was always clearer, and here in his lonely motel room he pondered those days leading to Kelly's decision. Perhaps he was to blame for wanting her to fit his mould. During the subsequent months her parents were the only people she contacted, and those occasions were sporadic at best.

Meanwhile, he'd accepted the situation but had mourned the loss of their friendship. He'd tried to repair the breach and had been somewhat successful. She was congenial whenever he called, but their camaraderie had disappeared. Awkwardness had taken its place. After a while he'd stopped trying to reach her.

As he turned onto his side a fresh wave of Mariah's scent drifted past his nose and he muttered a few choice words. Thanks to Burt's oversight in not sending a housekeeper to wipe out all traces of room ten's previous occupant, Andrew would pay the consequences all night long.

'I'm famished,' Nancy announced at mid-morning a week later. 'How about a break?'

Mariah's stomach growled, reminding her of the breakfast she'd skipped for a few minutes of extra sleep. 'I'll be along in a minute.'

After adding more samples to the chemistry analyzer's turntable, she followed Nancy into the lab's lounge and poured two cups of coffee. She passed one mug to her colleague who rested on the sofa, while happily munching a granola bar.

'You have a remarkable memory,' Nancy said between bites. 'I'm amazed you've worked yourself into the routine so quickly. It took me three months to feel comfortable. You're running circles around me after a few days.'

Mariah smiled. 'I was fortunate to be familiar with your instruments.'

Nancy finished her snack and stretched out her legs. 'I have to turn in our call-back schedule to the switchboard today. When would you like to start?'

'How long has it been since you've had a long weekend away from work?' Mariah countered.

Nancy grinned. 'I can't remember. Ancient history.'

'What does your husband think about your lack of free time?'

'Considering we've only been married six months, Jim's understandably unhappy. We need the income, though…' Nancy's voice trailed away. 'I keep praying for a med tech to move into town, but I don't hold out much hope. Gallup doesn't have the attractions of a big city so, unless someone with roots in the area wants a job, I doubt if our positions will be filled anytime soon. Didn't you say you came from a small town?'

Mariah hated to squelch the hope in Nancy's voice, but it was necessary. 'Yes, but I love to travel so the versatility of my job is perfect. I don't want to stay in one place for long.'

Nancy shrugged. 'I had to ask. Just in case.'

'I understand. As for the call schedule, I'll volunteer for this weekend.'

Nancy's expression was priceless—disbelief, hope and excitement flitted across her dainty features. 'I can't let you do that,' she protested. 'The Fourth of July is one of our busiest holidays. We have the usual emergencies plus all the firework-related injuries. It's rough enough for a seasoned person to handle, much less someone new.'

Mariah heard Nancy's disappointed note. 'Don't be ridiculous. You've already commented on how quickly I've caught on to your operation. If it will make you feel better, why don't you consider yourself as my back-up? I'll notify you if I need help.'

Nancy's face blossomed with anticipation once again. 'Before I'll agree, you must promise not to wait until you're totally swamped. If you've had a busy day I'll take over any night duty.'

'Fair enough. Why don't I take tonight as a trial run?'

'I have a better idea. We'll split the shift. You cover until ten o'clock and I'll take the remainder. That way, we'll both get a few hours of free time.'

'Great. As for the rest of the month, why don't you fit your hours around Jim's schedule and I'll handle the rest?'

Deep in a discussion on equal division of the call-time, neither woman noticed Polly at the doorway until the brusque secretary cleared her throat. 'Dr Prescott's ordered an a.s.a.p. prothrombin time in room one twelve.'

'I'll go. It's my turn.' Mariah swallowed the last sip of coffee and took Polly's note on her way out the door. 'Back in a flash.'

Taking the shortest route, she kept a sharp eye out for Dr Prescott. After their last memorable evening together she wanted to avoid him at all costs, and up to this point had been successful.

Considering herself an easygoing individual, she still couldn't believe she'd argued with him. Whenever she'd had a difference of opinion with someone, she'd always been able to articulate her position. Unfortunately, the situation with Kelly didn't allow her that luxury.

However, their disagreement wasn't as bothersome as the way she'd turned to mush in his embrace. For heaven's sakes, the man still loved his former fiancée. Once he learned about his daughter he wouldn't give Mariah a second thought.

Not that she was ready for his second or even his first thought. She simply refused to experience the pain of rejection on top of the grief she'd already endured.

A few minutes later she crossed the threshold of her destination. The pert eighty-year-old man stared at her with suspicion. 'If you're wantin' blood from me, you can visit someone else, missy. I've been poked and prodded so many times I ain't got none left.'

Mariah set her carryall on the table, taking no offence at the crusty fellow's gruff tone. Chronically ill patients often wearied of donating their blood to what often seemed a lost cause. 'Now, Mr Harper, I won't take it all. I'll leave some so I have an excuse to visit you again.'

Harper's faded blue eyes twinkled. 'Missy, are you flirting with me?'

She grinned. 'Of course. Have to stay in practice.'

'You oughta practise on someone closer to yer own age. Someone like our Dr Drew.' He cackled.

'I prefer older men,' she answered, hoping their voices didn't carry out of the room.

'I'll let you poke me but you'll have to pay for the privilege.'

She stifled a smile. 'What's the going rate these days?'

'A round of checkers.' He pointed to the box on the ledge.

'That could be quite a few games in the next couple of days,' she said, frowning.

He raised his chin, as if offering a dare. 'Take it or leave it.'

'You drive a hard bargain, Cal Harper.'

He gave her a toothy grin. 'You gotta play serious, too. No stupid moves.'

'Of course. After all, I'm out for blood.'

He guffawed. 'I can tell you're a good sort so I'll let you have the first bottle free. What're ya wantin' it for?'

Before Mariah could comment, a baritone interrupted.

'She's checking your blood thinner medication.' Andrew's long strides brought him into the room. 'We've done this before.'

Mariah hid her trepidation. This was the first time she'd seen him since they'd parted on unpleasant terms and she wasn't sure what to expect. To her relief, Andrew didn't toss her a second glance.

'Do you remember showing me your bruises?' Andrew asked Cal.

She prepared her equipment, noticing the reddish-purple blotching that marred the paper-thin skin on the old man's arms. The discoloration was an ominous sign of possible coagulation problems, she understood why Andrew had ordered the test a.s.a.p.

'Course I do. I just wanted to make sure *she*...' Harper pointed to Mariah '...knew what she was doin'.'

'I'll be careful,' Mariah promised. 'I can't afford to make a mistake at the price you're charging.'

Andrew's jaw dropped. 'You're *paying* him?'

'It's more of a deal. One checker game per needle-stick.'

Andrew's burst of laughter caught her by surprise. It was deep and hearty and made her want to hear it often. 'You old rascal. I'd better warn the nurses.'

Cal's faded blue eyes twinkled. 'Too late. I've already got three games on fer tonight, including one fer a back rub that I don't aim to lose. So, Drew. Are you gonna change my medicine?'

'I'll decide after I get these results.'

Mariah slid the needle into a vein that seemed the size of the Alaskan pipeline, pleased to hear Andrew's patient tone as he dealt with the old gentleman. Some physicians she'd encountered weren't as considerate, especially if they had to repeat their conversations as Andrew was obviously doing.

Before long she placed a cotton ball over the tiny

needle mark. 'Keep pressure on that for several minutes,' she instructed.

'OK.' He looked at Andrew. 'I won't have to be here long, right?'

'Just until your medication is stabilized,' Andrew said. He spoke to Mariah. 'How soon before I have a report?'

'About twenty minutes.' After a final check of Harper's arm, she said goodbye. 'See you later.'

'Without your needles,' the old man reminded her.

She smiled. 'Without my needles.'

Knowing her performance was under scrutiny, she returned to her section of the hospital at a fast clip.

Polly handed her a note. 'Nancy went to a meeting and you have an outpatient to see.'

'I'll take her in a minute.' Mariah placed Harper's tube in the centrifuge for its ten-minute spin cycle, then strode toward the waiting area. She recognized the name on the physician's orders, before addressing the only person she saw.

'Virginia Evers?'

'That's me.' A fifty-year-old brunette with silver highlights in her hair, wearing a calico skirt and matching red blouse, dropped her pile of knitting into a canvas tote bag before she rose. 'You're with TLC Inc, aren't you?'

News travelled fast in Gallup. 'Yes.'

'I usually wait for a copy of my results. I've signed all the release forms.'

'No problem. Come this way, please.' Mariah led her to the drawing station behind a moveable office partition around the corner.

Virginia sat in the chair and held out her arm. 'How's Kelly?'

Mariah pulled on a pair of gloves and disinfected the

bend of Virginia's elbow with alcohol. 'As far as I know, she's fine. Then again, I haven't talked to her for a while.'

Virginia sighed. 'She doesn't call home much either. She used to at first, but her dad…' Her voice trailed off. 'I guess she's busy, running from one job to the next.'

Mariah stopped herself from mentioning Kelly's preference for long-term assignments. 'There's plenty of work for us,' she replied instead, fixing her attention on her task of drawing blood. Unwilling to talk about Kelly in case Virginia reacted as vehemently as Andrew, she changed the subject.

'What are you knitting?'

A tiny smile flitted across Virginia's mouth. 'A baby blanket. It never hurts to have a few last-minute gifts on hand.' Her brown-eyed gaze met Mariah's and a silent understanding passed between them.

An ache built behind Mariah's eyes and a lump grew in her chest. If Virginia didn't know about Carlie she apparently had her suspicions.

Mariah cleared her throat. 'It's a good idea. My mom does the same thing. Now,' she said, reverting to business to regain her composure, 'if you'll wait outside, I'll have your CBC results shortly.'

'Thank you. I do hope my platelet count hasn't fallen. I can't bear to think about taking prednisone again. I suffer such terrible side-effects.'

'We'll know in a few minutes.'

Mariah fled, her logic conflicting with her heart. She didn't want to be in the middle of Kelly's problems—she had enough of her own. Although she forced herself to concentrate on the blood samples requiring her attention, inner turmoil raged.

It didn't help to see that Virginia's platelet count had dropped from her previous one.

She handed Virginia the written report. 'I'm afraid the result is lower this time.'

Virginia's mouth and shoulders drooped. With shaking hands she folded the page in half and slid it into her purse. She stiffened her spine with obvious effort. 'It's been worse.' She hesitated. 'Please don't tell my daughter. I don't want her to worry.'

All these secrets. 'I won't. But you should.'

Virginia hesitated. 'In due time. Anyway, if you talk to Kelly give her my love.'

'I will.'

A few minutes later Mariah called Cal Harper's protime result to the nurses' station. Preoccupied with the web of intrigue she'd inadvertently become entangled in, Andrew's voice caught her off-guard for a moment. 'Hmm, Harper's protime is fifty-five point two seconds.'

His voice sharpened. 'You sound strange. Is everything OK down there?'

'Peachy.' She wasn't about to admit that her brain had short-circuited or explain why.

As if mollified by her answer, he reverted to his professional tone. 'Repeat the protime in twelve hours, at ten p.m.'

'I will,' she promised. The normal range was around twelve seconds, while the therapeutic range for coumarin therapy was approximately two and a half times that figure. Harper's number exceeded the maximum and so he would be closely monitored until his results fell to acceptable levels.

'And you're OK,' he stated again.

'I'm fine. Thanks for asking,' she said politely, before

dropping the receiver into its cradle. Mental exhaustion flooded over her and she rubbed her temples.

The lines of communication between Kelly, her parents and Andrew had definitely been cut. It was becoming more and more clear that Mariah might be the only one who could repair them.

And yet she didn't want to become embroiled in anyone's personal problems. She had a job to do and she wanted to do it. Andrew was wrong. She wasn't hard-hearted—she'd simply isolated herself from future pain and disappointment. If she couldn't pull herself out of her own quandaries, how could she consider helping anyone else?

She slumped in her chair. This simple assignment was wreaking havoc with her conscience.

CHAPTER FIVE

MARIAH'S on-call status for the holiday weekend became official at four o'clock on Thursday. As three diabetics needed glucose checks before supper, Mariah spent the next hour wandering around the hospital to familiarize herself with its floor plan.

The hospital was built in a T-shape, with Surgery, Recovery and Intensive Care in the North wing, medical, surgical and the emergency wings in the East and the business offices in the third, or West wing. The nursery and obstetrics unit formed the branching point for the three sections. Departments like the lab and physical therapy were scattered along the longest corridor, facing south.

As she meandered down hallways, a sense of satisfaction filled her soul. Although she hadn't actually worked on the bench since she'd advanced to a management position a year ago, her skills hadn't left her. Barring an emergency requiring a blood transfusion, she could handle whatever medical situation arose.

At one point she hesitated at the nursery window. Three newborns were asleep, one happily sucking on a pacifier. Her maternal instincts surfaced and she pictured herself holding a brown-eyed, brown-haired baby. She'd always planned to have children—had even hoped that by now she would have.

At thirty-three, with no marital prospects in sight and a job that didn't allow her to cultivate long-term relationships, she obviously wasn't meant to be anything but career-minded.

She'd lost count of the number of times throughout the day when she'd questioned her decision to refuse Andrew's request. And yet, from a business standpoint, she'd taken the most beneficial route.

Beneficial for whom?

For TLC Inc, she told herself firmly. The company held her allegiance and she wouldn't forget it.

'Daydreaming, Ms Henning?'

The familiar baritone once again caught her by surprise. Had her thoughts been so apparent or did Andrew Prescott have an uncanny ability to read minds? 'Yes and no,' she prevaricated.

He raised one dark eyebrow but she didn't elaborate.

'I have a few tests to run at five so, rather than go home for an hour, I decided to stay. But, don't worry, I'm not padding my timesheet.'

'I'm glad to hear it.' He pointed to the row of bassinets and his tone softened. 'They're cuties, aren't they?'

Her gaze returned to the babies and this time she noticed one infant in particular. The tiny dark-haired girl had a serene look on her face as she slept with one hand curled next to her mouth. She read the pink card taped to the bed. 'Jenny Ross,' it read, along with all her vital statistics of length and weight, date and time of birth.

'I agree,' she answered. 'Especially Jenny Ross. I see you're listed as the doctor.'

'Yes,' he said proudly, his voice gentle. 'She's one of mine. I wish I'd kept a tally of all the babies I've delivered, but she was one of the easiest ones. Especially with a first-time mother.'

Once again she felt a distinct prick of her conscience—Virginia and Andrew deserved to know about Carlie. She changed the subject.

'How's the boy with the dog bite?'

'Travis is doing well but we've had to start the series of rabies vaccinations. Bill Townsend hasn't tracked down the dog's tag yet. The animal probably came from out of state.'

'Lost by a vacationer?'

'Or dumped,' he said. 'Sadly enough, it happens. By the way, Cal Harper thinks you're the best vampire he's ever met.'

She grinned. 'He's a nice man. I'm amazed he lives alone. Then again, he's awfully spry for being eighty.'

'He *was* spry,' Andrew said, 'until his car accident about six months ago. He lay pinned in the wreckage for several hours before a rescue crew could remove him. By the time he'd recovered from his injuries some weeks later he'd developed a thrombosis in his femoral vein. After heparin therapy, I'd switched to coumarin and he was doing well.'

'Thank goodness he recognized the bleeding under his skin.'

'He did, but he didn't appreciate its seriousness. He'd noticed it several days earlier, but waited to say or do anything until his home health agency nurse came for her visit. She's the one who brought him into ER.' He shook his head. 'Cal needs more supervision but he refuses to leave his home. He has a tendency to forget he's taken his pills so he takes them again. If one dose will work wonders, two will be better.'

'Is that what happened this time?'

Andrew nodded. 'His prescription should have lasted a month, but the bottle was nearly empty after two weeks.'

'Doesn't he have any family to look after him? Someone nearby?' As soon as she'd said the words she mentally cringed. Although Virginia Evers didn't require the level of care Cal Harper did, striking parallels existed between the two situations.

Andrew's eyes took on a cool glint as his mouth curved into a wry twist. 'He's a widower. No children. In any case, don't concern yourself. The people in this community look after their own.'

She refused to flinch under his frigid tone which would have revealed how much his comment stung. Yet she understood how he'd drawn his conclusion—she had come across as uncaring.

'I won't hold you up any longer,' he said stiffly. 'I know you have work to do.' He turned away, then pivoted to face her. 'I saw the schedule. Are you certain you're ready to work alone? And on a holiday weekend?'

'Absolutely.' Once again Mariah stood firm under his laser-like scrutiny.

'Our patients can't afford any mistakes.'

She chafed under his censure, but hid her irritation behind a calm expression. 'I know.'

He turned away. The next instant she blurted his name.

He stopped. 'Yes?'

Her impulsive plan to tell him that she was seriously considering his request died unspoken. Too many details had to be pieced together before she could claim success. She'd rather not raise his hopes, then explain her failure. 'Never mind. It was nothing.'

An hour and a half later, her work complete, she walked home. Seeing her neighbour, wearing a floppy straw hat as she tended her beds of yellow daffodils, Mariah stopped.

'Hello,' she called out. 'Your flowers are gorgeous.'

The woman sat back on her heels and smiled. 'Thank you.' She was in her late forties, and from the dirt smudges on her face and hands it seemed she totally enjoyed her hobby. After stripping off her soiled gardening gloves, she held out a hand. 'Rebecca Blackwell. My friends call me Becky.'

'Mariah Henning. I'm here for a few months.'

'At the hospital. Yes, I know.'

'You do?'

'This is a small town. Everything and anything is big news.'

Mariah motioned towards the flowers. 'How did you ever plant so many?'

Becky laughed. 'One at a time, my dear. One at a time. They don't normally last this long, but the weather's co-operated this year.'

'They'd make a lovely photograph.'

Becky smiled. 'They would. If I'm not mistaken, you're curious as to why I turned my yard into flowers.'

Mariah's face warmed.

'My husband loved daffodils. After he died I planted one for every day I knew him.'

'You must have known him a long time.'

'Since we were seniors in high school. He'd moved to town with his family and wasn't happy about being uprooted.' She giggled. 'He was terribly rude to everyone at first, but I wore him down.'

Mariah smiled. Already she could see that few people would be able to resist Becky's bubbly personality for long.

Becky surveyed her yard. 'My mother thought I was

crazy to plant so many, but I told her I'd rather plant flowers than sit in a shrink's office.'

'So it was therapeutic.'

'Best money I ever spent.' Becky rose, brushing the dirt off her knees. 'Let me know when you have a free evening. I'll show you around town.'

'I'd like that.'

'How's Andrew treating you?'

Warily, Mariah answered, 'Fine.' It wouldn't surprise her if the entire town knew of his aversion to her agency.

'If he doesn't, let me know. I babysat him when he was a little squirt so I know how to keep him in line. I'll even pass along a few tips if you need them.'

A deep, masculine laugh signalled Andrew's presence. 'Telling stories again, Becky?'

'Just the truth, Andrew,' she answered, her fondness for him evident. 'What can I do for you today?'

'Thought I'd see if you're still planting.'

'Nope. Planting's over. I'm tending now.' The distant ring of a telephone caught Rebecca's attention. 'Excuse me. I've been expecting a call. I hope this is it.' She dashed inside her house, the screen door slamming once behind her.

'I have to run, too.' Andrew's unnerving presence reminded Mariah of her own mission to contact Kelly. In fact, it had become a top priority.

To her surprise, Andrew fell into step beside her. 'Did everything run smoothly for you today?'

Still smarting from their last conversation, she resorted to a stiff politeness. 'Yes. Contrary to what you might think, I know my job.'

'So Nancy told me.' He hesitated. 'Have you had time to check out the town?'

'Not yet.' Obviously Nancy had laid his fears to rest

and he was trying to make peace. 'Becky's offered to take me around. She seems like a remarkable woman.'

'She is.'

'How long ago has she been alone?'

'About eighteen months. Ron was coming home late one night and had a flat tyre. While he was changing it another car came along and hit him. He died at the scene.'

Mariah fell silent, understanding Becky's pain all too well. And yet she marvelled at Becky's adjustment to her loss. If only Mariah could find a similar state of acceptance.

He stopped at the foot of the stairs and withdrew a white envelope from his shirt pocket. 'Before I forget, this came to me by mistake.'

She reached for the letter, her fingers brushing against his. While part of her mind marvelled at the heat and electricity surging up her arm, another part watched his arm yank away as if he'd touched a hot stove. The piece of mail fluttered to the ground like a giant snowflake.

He retrieved it for her, holding it by one corner.

Carefully accepting it, she glanced at the front. Her name appeared in block letters but the house number recorded underneath was Andrew's, not hers. Feeling somewhat sheepish, she stuck the envelope in the pocket of her scrub pants. She'd given her friend and fellow condo owner her Gallup address, and somewhere along the line Barbara had apparently written it down wrong.

'Thanks for bringing it over. I'll let my friend know about her error.'

He looked thoughtful, giving her a curt, dismissive nod before turning away.

Inside the kitchen her thoughts dwelt on the incident. The sparks arcing between them could have started a forest fire, but he'd appeared unshaken. His response rankled her feminine psyche, but at the same time Mariah found the idea troubling. How could she experience such an effect while her emotions remained tied to Dave?

After much thought, the answer popped into her head. The embers had only been a figment of her imagination. She didn't need to feel guilty. She hadn't betrayed Dave's memory. Clinging to that thought, she strode outside to relax in the porch swing as she ate a peanut butter and jelly sandwich. The evening air, laced with the scent of newly cut grass, smelled fresh and clean.

At twilight a car drove by at a leisurely pace, its headlights forming twin beacons on the paved street. She stared into the sky, picking out the constellations remembered from long-ago science classes. Crickets chirped and an occasional locust emitted its distinctive sound.

It was peaceful here. What a shame she couldn't say the same for her relationship with Dr Prescott. Working together amicably factored heavily in her work and it was becoming obvious that she'd never achieve such a state with him. Kelly would always be the wedge between them.

It would be best for everyone if Kelly accepted this assignment. Andrew would have what he wanted, Kelly's parents would be happy and Mariah could return to Denver and her VP position. If Kelly refused, however, Andrew would have to content himself with her answer. He looked after the interests of his patients while Mariah owed her allegiance to Kelly.

His accusation still rang in her ears like a church bell. Perhaps she and Kelly were guilty of running away from their problems. Neither had remained to make the best of bad circumstances. The similarities, however, ended there. Kelly wouldn't deal with her dilemma because she'd been in a no-win situation. Mariah, on the other hand, *couldn't* deal with hers because the pain was too great.

She twisted the ring on her left hand. It was time to stop running, to settle down, as her parents had suggested time after time. Unfortunately, knowing what she should do and putting it into practice were two different things. Even if she were ready to make another lifestyle change, she hadn't found the right place to call home. She hadn't made many friends during the past two years, at least not of the close variety. What had been the point? She was here today, gone tomorrow.

Like Dave.

Leaning her head against the backrest, she closed her eyes and waited for the familiar pain to take hold. It did, but for the first time it didn't seem as heart-wrenching. Either she was finally healing or she had become numb to its effects.

After this assignment she'd start looking for the perfect place to sink her roots. It would have to be a place where she'd be appreciated, a place where the physicians weren't judgemental or opinionated or stubborn.

The humour of her requirements struck her as she rose to telephone Kelly. Such places didn't exist.

'I'm sorry to call you at home on a holiday, but something's wrong with my Jimmy.' The phone line didn't disguise Helen Bleeker's trembling voice.

'What's the problem?' Andrew asked, picturing young James Bleeker as he cradled the phone against his shoulder and folded yesterday's newspaper. He remembered the boy because of his antics during weekly church services, rather than from seeing him in his office.

'He broke out with chickenpox a few days ago and was doing fine. I used calamine lotion for the itching and gave him acetaminophen for his fever. But tonight he's not acting right.'

Andrew's mental antenna rose. 'What do you mean?'

'Late this morning he started vomiting. As the day's gone on he's become more lethargic and more irritable. Sometimes he seems confused.'

With a diagnosis forming in his mind, he pulled himself to the edge of his easy chair. 'Take him to the ER immediately.'

'Isn't he still contagious?'

'Yes, but don't worry. I'll arrange for a room to be ready the moment you arrive. We'll check him out.'

'We'll be there in about ten minutes,' Helen said.

Andrew stretched as he rose and rubbed his face. His afternoon had been quiet for a Saturday, but the Bleeker case would occupy his evening.

He hunted for his shoes until he found them under the sofa. In a flash he slipped them over threadbare socks, which should have been retired but hadn't been because they matched his moss green twill trousers. A second later he was on his way.

Climbing into his vehicle, he glanced at Mariah's house. The front door was closed, the porch swing was motionless and her car sat in the driveway. He had a feeling she was still at the hospital because she gravitated to the swing whenever she was at home.

In any case, he would need her to assess Jimmy Bleeker's condition.

The moment Jimmy and his mother walked into ER, Bonnie directed them to an exam room. Andrew followed behind, noticing how the youngster trudged along—a mere shadow of the over-active child he remembered.

'You've got quite a few spots, Jimmy,' he remarked, noticing the red papules, vesicles and scabs indicative of the various stages of the rash on the boy's face, arms and torso, while Bonnie recorded his vital signs.

Jimmy nodded, his eyes droopy and lacking their usual sparkle.

Andrew listened to his heart and lungs, peered into his mouth and ears and glanced at the numbers in Bonnie's neat handwriting.

'Could he have ingested anything like insecticide or lead paint?'

Helen shook her head.

'And you've given him acetaminophen for the fever.'

'Yes. My husband gave him aspirin on the first day Jimmy broke out, but I switched because I've heard it's linked to Reye's syndrome.' Helen's eyes filled with panic. 'That isn't what he has, is it?'

'It's possible,' he admitted. 'He could also be suffering from a number of other conditions, including a form of poisoning. We'll know more after we do a few lab tests.' He turned to Bonnie. 'I'll want a CBC, a liver profile, a chem-six panel, a prothrombin time and a serum ammonia. Also a salicylate level. Stat.'

Bonnie nodded before she left the room on silent shoes. Andrew continued his examination of Jimmy's heart and lungs, mentally willing Mariah to arrive. Each passing moment and each observation he made pointed to the Reye's syndrome diagnosis, but he needed the numbers to confirm it.

A quiet woman's voice came over the loudspeaker. 'Three-three, call one-five.'

Out of habit, he deciphered the coded message—

Mariah was to contact the ER. He glanced at the clock. Where in the hell was she?

'I can't come back.' Kelly's normally cheerful voice sounded flat and lifeless.

Nearly twenty-four hours after her decision, Mariah had finally reached Kelly and presented her case. Pressing the point after Kelly's refusal seemed like treading on dangerous ground, but Virginia Evers's downcast face appeared in her mind's eye. 'Your mother would love to spoil Carlie.'

Kelly's sharp intake of breath corroborated Mariah's theory. 'You haven't told anyone about her, have you?'

'No,' Mariah said gently. 'But she's why you left Gallup in the first place, isn't she?'

Kelly sniffled. 'My father would have thrown me out, anyway. Or forced me into marrying Andrew.'

'You don't want to marry him?' Mariah struggled to keep her voice even while her thoughts regarding the woman's sanity raced.

'Andrew and I have been friends for a long time. Since we had a lot in common, we more or less drifted together until he finally proposed.'

Mariah couldn't imagine drifting into anything with Andrew. He was too forceful a man to settle for such a casual relationship.

'Carlie needs her father.' It pained her to say it.

'Not if he isn't father material,' Kelly said sharply.

Mariah's jaw dropped. The woman was absolutely certifiable.

'I was afraid to stay. Andrew and my dad are both used to getting their way, and they'd eventually wear me down. So, rather than fight them, I hunted for another job, using the excuse of trying my wings before I thought about marriage. Luckily, you hired me.'

Mariah hesitated. 'You'll have to tell your family some time. Andrew and your parents deserve the truth.'

'I know they do, but I can't.'

'Suppose something happens to you? Where will Carlie go?'

Kelly fell silent and Mariah continued. 'Shouldn't they hear about your daughter from you rather than someone else? And wouldn't you rather be in control of the situation when you break the news?'

Kelly sighed. 'I suppose.'

'As for being forced into something you don't want, you've been strong enough to create a new way of life without anyone's help. Don't sell yourself short now.'

The silence on the line suggested that Kelly was considering Mariah's arguments. Finally, Kelly's voice came across the miles. She sounded resigned. 'I'll come to Gallup, but I need time to make arrangements.'

Mariah wanted to shout her success, but she forced herself to be calm. 'Your current contract ends in six weeks. I'll see you then.'

With that settled, Mariah broke the connection. She leaned back in her chair, feeling drained. Andrew would be thrilled to hear of her success, and Virginia Evers's excitement at meeting her baby granddaughter would know no bounds.

She'd also pared down her stay in Gallup from six months to six more weeks. That alone was quite an accomplishment for a ten-minute phone call.

All in all, it was a good thing she was leaving sooner than anticipated. She didn't want to become emotionally entangled with a man who eagerly anticipated a reunion with another woman.

'Where have you been?' Andrew demanded as soon as Mariah reached the ER.

'In the lab. On the phone. I have some interesting news for you.'

'It'll have to wait. I have a possible Reye's syndrome. Seven-year-old boy.' He started toward the closest exam room. 'Hope you've had chickenpox.'

'Ages ago.'

He recited his list of lab orders, finishing with, 'Call Nancy if you need help because I want this as your top priority.'

'I understand.' Although she had completed her other tasks, she didn't take time to explain.

Andrew opened the door. Inside the confines of the small room, Mariah greeted the child with a smile, noting the eruptions on his face and arms and his general lack of animation. He reminded her of the cartoon character Dennis the Menace, down to the recalcitrant lock of blond hair.

Right now, however, he was one sick little boy.

'I'm going to take some blood from you, Jimmy,' she said, assembling her equipment and tubes. 'It won't take long.'

'Is it gonna hurt?' Jimmy asked in a plaintive note.

'About like a mosquito bite,' she said cheerfully, tugging on a pair of latex gloves. 'It won't be as bad as when you skinned your leg.'

He looked down at the long scrape, the edges puckered from the healing scabs. 'That's good.'

'How did you hurt your leg?' Drawing a child's attention away from the upcoming procedure often helped. She hoped the rule would apply now as Andrew's watchful eye focused upon her.

'Fell off my bike. I'd've beat Shelley, too, if I hadn't hit some sand.'

'Maybe next time. Make a fist for me, OK?' She slid the needle into his vein, pleased to see that he hardly flinched. 'Spend a lot of time outdoors?'

He nodded, closing his eyes. His strength was obviously ebbing. Even the blond cow-lick on his head seemed to droop.

She finished, taping a cotton ball over the site. After labelling the tubes and gathering her things, she patted his arm. 'You did great. My best patient ever.'

A tiny smile tugged at the corners of his mouth.

Mariah pressed a special 'I had my blood drawn' sticker to his shirt. 'See you later.'

Without waiting for Jimmy's reply, Mariah brushed past Andrew on her way to the door. His terse command was delivered in a tone meant for her ears only.

'I'll be waiting in ER.'

The worry in his eyes made her forgive him for his arrogance and impatience.

In spite of a fatigue borne of overwork and hunger, she raced to the lab. Working in an established rhythm, she performed the procedures one by one. Slowly, but surely, a picture of Jimmy's condition developed.

His liver enzymes were elevated, as was his serum ammonia and his protime—all indicative of liver involvement.

She dialed ER's extension and reported her findings over the telephone to Bonnie. Her obligations met, she decided to take time for a break before she collapsed.

Luckily she'd had the foresight to create a stockpile of non-perishable foods in their lounge. She selected a can of orange juice out of the apartment-sized refrigerator and took a long swallow.

Her stomach reminded her of the meal she hadn't finished at noon so she poured hot water into a styrofoam container of oriental noodles. While waiting for the three minutes' preparation time to pass, she propped her feet on a chair and closed her eyes.

'Don't tell me you're going to eat that?' Andrew said from the doorway.

Startled, she dropped her feet to the floor. 'Eat what?'

He pointed to her supper.

Mariah shrugged. 'Beats going without.'

He pointed to a stainless-steel pot on the warmer. 'Any coffee left?'

'It's hot water. Help yourself to the instant.'

After making his drink in the only clean mug, he pulled out a chair from under the table and sank down with a sigh.

'How's Jimmy?' she asked.

'It looks like Reye's. His liver enzymes are abnormal but the bilirubin is OK, his glucose is at the low end of the expected range and his ammonia is high. The infectious disease specialist in Casper agrees.'

'What's his treatment?'

He drank part of his coffee. 'Mainly supportive, along with managing the cerebral oedema. Because of the liver damage, he's on IV fluids with glucose at two-thirds of maintenance level, an antibiotic, a diuretic and vitamin K to counteract the lower production of clotting factors.'

'Then you caught his condition in time?'

'I hope so,' he said fervently, staring into the bottom of his mug. 'He's at a Stage I now, but we'll have to be alert for symptoms of progression.'

'Which are?' she prompted.

'Seizures, coma, death.' He paused. 'According to the textbooks, if the initial ammonia level is greater than one hundred, using our units of measurement, progression to the higher stages can be anticipated.'

'But Jimmy's level wasn't that high.'

'No, but I don't want to risk his condition deteriorating. The disease has a thirty per cent fatality rate.'

'So you'll send him to another facility.'

Five o'clock shadow rasped as Andrew rubbed his face. 'I want to, but his father doesn't believe his son's ill enough to warrant a transfer. He bragged to me about how his boy bounces back quickly every time he's sick. I couldn't convince him that Reye's isn't like a sore throat or a common cold.'

Andrew slapped his mug against the table. 'The child needs more than we—than I—can give him here. Intracranial pressure monitoring for one. I don't want to wait until the specialists can't save him either.'

His anguish and frustration were palpable and Mariah's heart went out to him. 'So, what will you do?'

'The only things I can do. I'll repeat his ammonia, glucose and serum osmolality in four hours. After I fax those results to the specialist, we'll see.' He drained the last of his coffee. 'It'll be a long night for you.'

She shrugged. 'For you, too.'

He rose. 'If you go home, be careful.'

'Thanks for the warning, but I'll probably stay here until Jimmy's either stabilized or shipped out.' She took a bite of her noodles, then frowned. They tasted like the paper container.

He laughed at her expression. The lines on his face softened. 'Didn't you mention that you had something to tell me?'

She remembered. 'Yes, I did.'

'And?'

Mariah took a deep breath. 'Kelly's agreed to come back. Temporarily, of course.'

His face lit up like the proverbial Christmas tree. 'When?'

'In six weeks. After she finishes her contract.'

'Can't you release her—?'

Mariah was adamant. 'No. Besides, she needs time to…' Her mind raced for a plausible excuse. 'She needs time to make arrangements.'

'What's to arrange? All she needs to do is throw her clothes in a suitcase.'

Mariah wasn't about to be trapped into saying something she'd regret. 'Be glad she's coming. Period. Don't forget, I'm still trying to operate a business and Kelly has commitments.'

'You're right.' He leaned in his chair until his weight rested on the two back legs, looking as excited as a teenage boy preparing for his first date. Mariah tried not to dwell on why it bothered her.

'We need to celebrate,' he said, repositioning himself so all four chair legs touched the floor.

She pushed her styrofoam cup of noodles closer. 'Be my guest. I'm willing to share.'

He shook his head. 'No. Something special.'

Mariah wondered if he'd celebrate when she left town. 'If you're hinting for champagne, you're out of luck. We're both on duty.'

'Pizza. That's what we need. In fact, it'll be my treat.'

'Sounds good to me. It's an improvement over flavoured instant noodles.'

He reached for the phone at the opposite end of the table, then punched a number from memory. His deep voice sent a shiver down Mariah's spine and, oddly enough, she felt unsettled and awkward.

'Forty-five minutes,' he said. 'The delivery people will leave it at the front desk.'

'Fine.'

Andrew snapped his fingers. 'Have you called her parents?'

'No. Kelly probably will.'

He shook his head in disbelief. 'She's coming home. I can hardly believe it.'

'Believe it.'

'You know something? This is the best news I've heard all day.'

'I'm glad,' she said, jealous of her employee. Suddenly six weeks of watching Andrew eagerly await Kelly's arrival seemed cruel and unusual punishment.

Andrew smiled as he imagined Virginia Evers's reaction to the news. The woman who'd been like his second mother hadn't been her vivacious self since Kelly had moved away. Her disease had played a role, but losing her daughter factored more heavily in her depressed emotional state than her illness. Most people hadn't noticed because she'd managed to hide her turmoil, but he had. Winston had even drawn him aside a few months ago and expressed his concern. Thanks to Mariah Henning, Virginia's mood would improve.

Thanks to Mariah. His own thought echoed through his brain. Her apparent change of heart had seemed out of character and yet—was it? He studied her face, charting the lines exhaustion had etched on her smooth forehead and noticing her mouth's tired droop. Watching her aimlessly stir the container's contents with a plastic spoon, he knew that he'd misjudged her. It was almost as if she'd wanted him to think the worst, but if so her actions didn't make sense.

She glanced at him then began to fidget, as if aware

she had captured his undivided attention. 'Is there a noodle on my face?' she quipped.

He shook his head, keeping his gaze fixed. 'You didn't have to call Kelly, but you did. What made you change your mind?'

She took a long swallow of juice. 'Woman's prerogative.'

'Really,' he said, sounding unconvinced as he folded his arms across his chest.

'It was strictly a business decision.'

'Ah, yes. Business.'

'It was,' she insisted.

'I wasn't disagreeing,' he said, recognizing her attempt to camouflage her soft spot. She'd probably hidden behind this defence mechanism since her fiancé died. An inward satisfaction began to grow. Mariah wasn't the barracuda he'd thought she was—she'd simply pretended to be one.

'I received word of a cancellation so Kelly lost her next assignment. It wasn't logical for me to juggle my TLC Inc responsibilities with Gallup Memorial's while Kelly had none. Since you'd made your wishes plain, I asked her to consider filling in for me.'

He pursed his lips. 'Did she *want* to come?'

Mariah's gaze lowered in what Andrew deemed a guilty fashion. 'She agreed to take my place. That's what's important, isn't it?'

Something about Mariah's evasive answer raised his alert flags. As he pondered her response a startling idea occurred to him. She was protecting Kelly, but he couldn't imagine why.

CHAPTER SIX

EXPECTING to see Jimmy asleep, Mariah entered his room at nine o'clock as quietly as she could. His mother and older brother were in the room and both jolted upright at her appearance. Mariah attributed their guilty expressions to being caught, sitting on Jimmy's bed.

She placed her tray on the bedside table. 'I'm here for another blood sample, I'm afraid.'

Mrs Bleeker stepped aside, then motioned for her son to do the same. 'I didn't realize it was that time again.'

'It'll only take a minute,' Mariah promised. She bent over Jimmy. 'Hi, Jimmy. I brought my mosquito back. He wants some more blood.'

He nodded, groggy but content.

However, as Mariah repositioned his arm on top of a small blanket someone had brought from home Jimmy's eyes flew open. A mass next to his chest wriggled, then let out a sigh.

'What in the—?'

Mariah pulled back the sheet to find a puppy, snoring away, snuggled against its owner. She glanced at the door, relieved to see it was closed. 'How did you sneak him in here?' she whispered.

Jimmy's brother, an older tow-headed version of his younger brother, looked cocky. 'It's not a him. It's a her. Smuggled her in, wrapped in Jimmy's blanket.'

'Rickie will take him home, but we thought Jimmy might rest easier if he could see Sniffles,' Mrs Bleeker added. 'And he has.'

'I'm glad, but I don't think the nursing staff will be too happy to find his dog here.'

Rickie frowned as he struck a belligerent pose. 'Seeing-eye dogs can go anywhere people go. I checked.'

'Yes, but I don't think Sniffles qualifies,' Mariah said gently.

'Dogs go into nursing homes, too,' Rickie said defensively. 'They help the old people relax. One of our *Weekly Reader* magazines had a whole article on it.'

'I know, but not everyone is as open-minded about this as we are. Why don't we keep this episode to ourselves?' Mariah suggested. 'If anyone asks, I didn't see or hear a thing. OK?'

Satisfied, the boy nodded. Jimmy grinned.

As Mariah took his blood sample she had a thought. 'Do you have a photograph? Jimmy can look at Sniffles all the time and you won't have to worry about being caught.'

Rickie shook his head.

'No problem. I'll take one for you.' The words escaped her before she could recall them.

'Will you?' Jimmy's voice sounded weak.

Mariah nodded. 'I'll be back in about an hour. Think you can hide him that long?'

Rickie's eyes brightened. 'You bet.'

Hurrying from the room, Mariah wondered if she could be fired over ignoring a dog in a patient's room. At the very least she'd receive a counselling memo in her file. She chuckled. After seeing the sheer contentment on Jimmy's face, she didn't care.

By the time she arrived in the lab, the blood was clotted and ready for the centrifuge. Ten minutes later she pipetted the serum into a sample cup, dropped it into a numbered slot and pressed the analyzer's start button.

Andrew appeared in the doorway. 'I came to ask if you have the Bleeker boy's results.'

'I'm running his tests now. It'll be a few more minutes.' She moved aside to another small instrument, placed a drop of the serum on the test pad, then closed the door.

'Jimmy seemed about the same to me,' she commented.

'He isn't any worse. We're trying to keep his glucose high and his ammonia low. I hope we've been successful.' He tapped his foot. 'How much longer?'

The sound of paper advancing and the crackling noise of a printer caught her attention. 'This should be it.' She walked to the instrument and wondered once again why it had been installed in a corner with so little manoeuvring room.

He followed her to peer over her shoulder. Mariah felt his breath on her neck and she forced away a shiver—a shiver that had nothing to do with fear and everything to do with him standing only centimetres away. His familiar masculine scent wafted into her nostrils. An image of Andrew reaching for her formed, his arms curling around her while he nuzzled his face in her neck...

Reality intruded. 'His glucose is slightly elevated. One thirty-five.'

'I wanted it closer to one fifty.'

She moved away to another workstation, grateful for an excuse to add distance and allow herself time to recover before she made a fool of herself. After all, Kelly consumed his interest. 'His ammonia hasn't dropped.'

He squared his jaw. 'I can't wait to send him to another hospital. He needs to go now.'

'Have his parents agreed?'

'They'd better, or I'll get a court order to override their wishes.' With that, he strode away.

Mariah sent up a silent prayer for the Bleekers to see reason. Realizing that time was wasting before her own appointment, she hastily stored her reagents and supplies, then dashed home.

Disregarding neatness, she dug through her box of photographic supplies for her old Polaroid camera. As if fate was lending a hand, she found a package of in-date film. Armed with the Polaroid, as well as her more professional thirty-five millimetre camera, she rushed back to the hospital.

Fortunately, the corridors were deserted and she slipped inside Jimmy's room unnoticed.

The strain on the faces, staring back at her, was evident and the family greeted her with relief.

Mariah positioned the puppy next to Jimmy, noticing how the dog snuggled against its master. She snapped the Polaroid's shutter, and while the photograph developed before their eyes she took several more shots, using the other camera. Those pictures would require developing in a photo lab, and with any luck one would be suitable for enlarging.

'All done,' she murmured. While Rickie placed Sniffles inside his jacket, she handed the instant picture to Jimmy. 'Now you'll have Sniffles with you all the time.'

Jimmy pressed the picture to his chest and closed his eyes, wearing a smile. Tears of gratitude welled in Mrs Bleeker's eyes. 'I don't know how to thank you.'

'His recovery is all the thanks I need,' Mariah said, struggling with her own bout of emotion. She couldn't bear to think of the vibrant little boy becoming one of the dreaded thirty per cent.

Muted voices caught her attention and an instant later the door swung open. As Andrew and one of the nurses walked in, Rickie slipped into the corridor without a word of protest. Mariah felt Andrew's gaze land first on her, then on the equipment slung over her shoulder. Trapped in the corner, she couldn't leave although she didn't belong here.

He addressed Mrs Bleeker. 'I've called LifeWatch to take him to the medical centre in Casper. They'll be here in ten minutes.'

She nodded as she stroked her son's cheek with the back of her fingers. 'He's always been so full of life. I remember how I'd wonder if he would ever sit still. Now...' her voice trembled '...I wonder if he'll ever be my rambunctious boy again.'

Mariah blinked rapidly and she fidgeted with the straps on her camera case.

Mrs Bleeker glanced at Andrew, a tear balanced on the edge of one eyelash. 'Tell them to take good care of my son. I can't lose him.'

Andrew cleared his throat and his eyes appeared moist. 'The staff in Casper are the best. They'll fight for him as much as we would.'

Mariah always wondered how physicians could deal with serious situations and be unaffected. She saw first-hand how their professional demeanour was simply an act. She didn't envy them the task of breaking bad news to family members.

'There should be room for you if you want to fly with him,' he added.

Her face brightened. 'I do.'

'If you need to make arrangements you'd better hurry. The flight crew won't wait.'

Mrs Bleeker rushed away in search of her husband.

Mariah headed toward the hallway, but Andrew's voice stopped her at the door.

'Don't leave, Mariah. We may need you.'

She nodded, then raced to the lab to deposit her cameras and grab her carryall of supplies. To save time, she waited in the nurses' station for further instructions.

Andrew walked out of Jimmy's room and sank onto an empty chair beside her. 'Have you left the hospital at all today?'

'I think so. Or maybe that was yesterday.' She shrugged. 'I'll go home soon enough.'

While he scribbled in the chart, Mariah went to Jimmy's side. She hated the thought of him being alone so she sat near his bed until his mother returned.

The next half-hour passed quickly. The LifeWatch crew arrived, assessed Jimmy's condition and bundled him off to the helipad.

Mariah stood outside the range of the lights glaring into the night. She should have gone home—her work was over—but she felt compelled to remain until the helicopter lifted off for the next leg of the journey.

Andrew spoke to Mrs Bleeker, helped her inside and then stood back while the pilot slammed the door.

He joined Mariah and together they watched the helicopter's blades accelerate to a steady whir before the machine left the ground. Its blinking lights and an acrid smell of smoke, drifting along the summer breeze, reminded her of the holiday's events.

'We missed the fireworks,' she said.

'So we did. Better luck next year.'

She wouldn't be back, but didn't say so. 'Time to go home,' she said instead.

'I'll give you a ride.' He spoke casually, masking his ulterior motive to satisfy his curiosity about this paradoxical woman. Grilling her while she was exhausted could be construed as underhanded tactics, but it seemed the only way he might obtain any answers.

'I'm too tired to refuse. Thanks.'

He guided her toward his vehicle with a hand at her waist. She hadn't stiffened under his touch, reinforcing his belief that her natural defences were down.

Her light scent and soft skin reminded him of his self-imposed monkish existence—a lifestyle he was eager to remedy.

Before long he accompanied her up her porch steps. She reached to open the door, but he forestalled her. 'Don't go. Not yet.'

'What's on your mind?' she asked, stifling a yawn.

'You are.'

She blinked. 'I am?'

Andrew nodded. 'I have a question to ask you.'

'Go ahead. I don't have any secrets.'

'Jimmy barely let go of his photograph long enough for me to look at it,' he said, his eyes watching for her reaction. 'He told me it was his dog.'

'He's attached to Sniffles.'

'I could tell it was taken in his hospital room. More specifically, his hospital bed.'

'You don't say.' She sounded innocent—*too* innocent.

'The question is—who smuggled a puppy into the hospital and how did they do it?'

'Beats me.'

He grinned. 'The nurses will throw a fit when they find the evidence. Dogs shed, you know.'

Mariah threw up her hands. 'Honestly! Patients and family members these days just can't follow the rules. No smoking, no pets, no visiting after hours.'

'Apparently, our staff can't either.'

'Surely you're mistaken.'

His laugh came from deep inside. 'You won't admit to being part of the escapade, will you?'

She smiled. 'Would you if you were in my shoes?'

'No.' He paused, his mood turning serious. 'I want to know one thing, though.'

'What's that?'

'You're not as hardhearted as I'd thought. Are you?'

Mariah shrugged, as if uncomfortable under his scrutiny. 'It depends. Everything is relative, you know.'

He ran his fingertips along her jaw line, feeling her tremble under his feather-light caress. Her response satisfied his masculine ego. 'You're a fake, Mariah Henning.'

'What makes you say that?' Sounding breathless, she stumbled over her words.

Andrew stared at lips begging for his personal attention. 'A die-hard business woman wouldn't take time to play checkers with an old man.'

'I like checkers,' she countered.

He continued as if she hadn't interrupted. 'Nor would she bend the rules to photograph a sick child's puppy.'

'I'm thinking about entering another contest.'

'Sorry, but I don't buy that story either. You're the most intriguing female I've ever met.'

'You can't know many women.'

'I've always prided myself on my ability to judge people's characters. Lately, it seems I'm not as good as I once thought. First Kelly, now you.'

'Perhaps you saw what you wanted to see.'

He stepped back to lean against the railing. 'Could be. Kelly had been part of my life for so long that it didn't seem right to let our dreams die a natural death.'

'No matter how badly we want them,' she said, her

voice sounding distant, 'some dreams aren't meant to become reality.'

Realizing that Mariah spoke from experience, he nodded. 'I'd have done anything for her.'

After a brief hesitation Mariah asked, 'And now?'

'We've been friends for too long. I couldn't turn my back on her if she needed me. If she's in trouble...' he held Mariah's gaze to emphasize his point '...I'll do what I can to help her straighten out her life.'

'Who said she was in trouble?'

'No one. You asked a hypothetical question and I gave you a hypothetical answer.'

'I see.'

'I'm not certain you do,' he said, moving toward her to cup her chin in his hand. 'In time, you will.' With that, he placed his mouth against hers. To his delight, she trembled in his arms. Regretfully he released her a moment later. 'Mark your calendar. We have a date for the next Fourth of July holiday.'

She appeared stunned for a few seconds before she recovered. 'I never plan more than a few months ahead. One day at a time is my motto.'

'You need a new one.'

'If you think of something, let me know,' she quipped.

He smiled. 'I will. Count on it.'

I'd have done anything for her...I couldn't turn my back on her. Andrew's words echoed in Mariah's head for over a week. If she had any doubts about what would happen once he saw Kelly, with Carlie in tow, they now fled. Even if he felt something special for Mariah, his feelings for Kelly and his child would override all others.

Eager to escape her depressing thoughts, she went to

visit Cal Harper. 'How're you doing this afternoon?' she asked upon entering his room.

He quirked one white eyebrow, resignation written on his aged features. 'I suppose you're wanting more blood.'

'Nope. I'm going to bother someone else, but I wanted to challenge you to a game of checkers first. Put some credit on my account.' She grinned.

'Aw, I ain't in the mood.'

She perched on the edge of the chair beside his bed. 'Not in the mood?' she said. 'This is coming from a man who keeps a board ready to go at a moment's notice? What's wrong?'

'Little Cindy Carpenter came in today and told me I'm gonna have to go to Sunny Acres. She says I can't take care o' myself any more. Says I need "assisted living", whatever that means.' He folded his arms across his chest. A distinctly mulish set came to his bony jaw.

'I knew Cindy when she was just a glimmer in her daddy's eye. Now she's tellin' me what I can and can't do. It just ain't right. So I'm a little forgetful. I get around pretty good. I don't need no assistance.'

'Maybe someone can move in with you.'

'Can't find nobody.' He sighed. 'It's the way of the world nowadays. Still, it don't mean I gotta like it.'

Mariah's heart went out to the man. How difficult it must be for him to accept the limitations of his body while his spirit remained so independent. Her grandmother had been the same way. Luckily she had had Mariah's parents to look after her. Cal had no one.

'Sunny Acres is a nice place or so I've heard. Just think of all the people available for checkers.'

'I s'pose.' He patted her hand. 'Run along, missy. I

know you have more important things to do than sit here, jawing with me.'

Her time was up, but she was hesitant to leave. 'Do you know when you'll go?'

'Nope, but I expect it'll be in a day or two.' He sighed. 'I'll miss my place. I loved to sit outside and hear the old windmill creak and the leaves rustlin' on the oak tree. I hope they'll let me go home one last time to say goodbye.'

'I'm sure they will. If not, let me know,' she said fiercely. 'I'll take you myself.'

'Thanks, missy. I'll keep it in mind.'

Choking with emotion, Mariah fled from the room. She understood the importance of keeping memories alive so before Cal went to Sunny Acres she'd make sure he had a piece of his home to take with him. It was the least she could do.

Nancy was on call tonight so Mariah intended to take advantage of her freedom. She rushed from the hospital to the local market for film, then home to change into a pair of denim shorts and a sleeveless plaid shirt.

With her thirty-five millimetre over one shoulder, and a Thermos of her favorite Irish mocha coffee in hand, she bounded down the porch steps toward her car. She'd planned to ask the gas station attendant for Cal Harper's address, but Andrew pulled into his drive at that moment and she changed her mind.

She tapped on his window before he stopped the engine. 'I'm looking for Cal Harper's place. How do I get there?'

He unfolded himself from his vehicle, his surprise evident. 'Hello yourself. Why do you want to see Cal's ranch?'

'He's checking into Sunny Acres. I want to take a few pictures for him.'

'So he told you.'

'Yes. He wasn't happy about it either.'

Andrew grimaced. 'I know. I wish it could be different, but—' He broke off. 'His house is hard to find unless you know where you're going.'

'Which is why I'm asking for directions,' she said, pointing out the obvious.

'I'll take you.'

According to her grandmother, time spent arguing was time wasted. 'Fine. Let's go.'

Andrew grinned. 'Can I change my clothes and grab something to eat first? I missed lunch to deliver a baby.'

'You'll have to hurry. I don't want to lose the light.' She glanced at the height of the sun and then at her watch. 'If it's all the same to you, I'll fix a sandwich for you to eat on the way.'

'Fair enough.'

Mariah scampered across the lawn. Ten minutes later she returned with a small ice chest filled with two cans of Pepsi, a small bag of seedless red grapes and two thick roast beef sandwiches with all the trimmings.

He met her near the kerb and relieved her of the ice chest. 'We'll take my truck. Last I heard, the road isn't in the best condition.'

'If you say so.' She climbed into the passenger side and fastened her seat belt. Glancing around the interior, she found everything in pristine condition. Thank goodness he'd volunteered his Land Cruiser for their trek— her car was neat, but a fine layer of dust covered the dashboard and the floor mats needed a good vacuuming.

'How do you keep your truck so clean?' she asked as

they headed west, picking up speed as they left town. 'When do you find the time?'

He grinned. 'Two boys down the street have an entrepreneurship, complete with business cards. In fact, I'm surprised they haven't contacted you. They're always looking for new clients.'

'I'm impressed.'

'You should be. It's quite an undertaking for a ten-and twelve-year-old.' He turned off the main highway, then took a series of dirt roads, each one progressively less deserving of the title. 'We're almost there.'

She eyed the narrow track with its deep ruts. 'Isn't the county responsible for maintenance?'

'Only for public thoroughfares. This is on Cal's property.'

Andrew slowed to a crawl and steered around the worst of the potholes created by years of neglect. He hit one bump and her camera slid off the seat and onto the floor.

'Sorry about that,' he said. 'I hope nothing broke.'

'Me, too.' Mariah unsnapped the seat belt to reach for her equipment, but a split second later she felt herself being thrown in the air like a rag doll.

She flung her arms outwards to grab something solid. Andrew braked and she found herself plastered against him, her hands clutching his biceps in a death grip.

His breath caressed her cheek and for a moment she could hardly breathe. 'Ready to go on?' he asked.

Loosening her hold, she nodded. Like a boxer retreating to his corner, she slid towards her side of the cab. She didn't get far.

'Stay in the middle,' he ordered, leaning across her to fix the centre seat belt in place.

His arm rested against her breast and the contact drove

the air out of her lungs. Time seemed to stand still as she waited for the audible click of metal.

He moved away. 'All set?'

She held the camera on her lap and managed a smile. 'I think so.'

'Good. Hang on.' He changed gears and the Land Cruiser moved forward.

For the next quarter of a mile she bounced along until she accepted the inevitable and used him as an anchor. He didn't say a word, but the corners of his mouth twitched into a smile.

Unwilling to break his driving concentration, she listened to a Garth Brooks tape and wondered how Andrew retained such hard biceps in his profession. Then, again, he admitted to owning a ranch. Perhaps he pitched in with chores when time permitted.

Finally he drove into a small clearing. 'Here we are.'

Mariah stared at the two-storey clapboard house. The roof had lost several shingles and the rest were in need of replacement. The wide wrap-around porch, encompassing the front and two sides, sagged in several spots. A few wooden shutters hung drunkenly in place and several window panes were cracked. Overall, the structure needed several coats of fresh paint.

She hopped out of the truck and meandered towards the porch. Cal liked to spend hours surveying his domain from this spot and she intended to photograph the view for him.

Andrew shortened his strides to match hers. 'Watch out for the loose boards,' he said, following her up the stairs.

'I will.' Standing at the railing, she saw the windmill and the oak tree Cal had mentioned, as well as a weathered red barn in comparatively good condition.

She saw dandelions, buffalo grass and a deep indentation in front of the barn that probably became a large puddle after rain. Imagining how the site appeared during each season, she understood Cal's reluctance to leave it for Sunny Acres.

'This is a beautiful place,' she commented, unslinging her camera from her shoulder to peer through the viewfinder.

'If you like this, I'll take you to my ranch.'

She paused to glance at him. 'You will?'

'Sure. I have a great pond in the pasture. Plenty of wildlife to see, if you're patient.'

'I'd like that. Help yourself to the food while I work.'

'Have you eaten?'

'Not yet, but I will. Later.'

'Then I'll wait, too.'

'Suit yourself.' Unselfconsciously, she began snapping the shutter, changing her location and lens angle for a variety of shots. By the time the light began to fade she'd taken three rolls of film.

'There should be a few good ones in that bunch,' she said, satisfied with her efforts.

'Have you always been a camera buff?'

She nestled her equipment back in its case before she sat on the wooden porch step. 'I started in ninth grade while working on the school paper. I preferred taking pictures to writing articles so my adviser let me concentrate on the photographic aspect. I worked hard to capture a special moment, an emotion, that revealed more than what could be written.'

'A picture being worth a thousand words?' he quipped, handing her a sandwich before lowering himself beside her.

'That's right. I entered a number of amateur contests and even won a few times.'

'What's your favourite subject?'

Mariah paused to think. 'It depends on my mood. Kids and pets are fun. I prefer candid shots, not the posed variety.'

He motioned to the surroundings. 'And scenery.'

'Yes, but not just any scenery. Scenery like this...' she waved her arms '...has character. I can't help but look at that old barn and wonder how many people were involved in its construction, if they had a barn dance when they finished—that sort of thing.'

He stared into the distance and nodded, as if he saw the same things she did. 'You look beyond the surface.'

'I try.'

A dog's bark drifted across the field. 'Where will you go when you leave Gallup?'

'My home base is in Denver. I'll be there for a few weeks before I go back on the road. I visit the facilities who have contracts with us, participate in job fairs—that sort of thing.'

'Do you plan to settle down? To stop living out of a suitcase?'

'You sound like my mother,' she teased. 'She asks me that question every time I talk to her.'

'She's probably worried about you. What do you tell her?'

Mariah met his gaze. 'That I will. Someday. When the conditions are right.'

'And what constitutes the right conditions?'

CHAPTER SEVEN

ANDREW was fishing—Mariah recognized the signs. 'It's more a combination of conditions—a friendly community, interesting people, a challenging job.'

'I'm surprised you haven't found such a place.'

'I haven't been looking. I'm satisfied with what I'm doing.' But even as she spoke disquiet nudged her. In actuality, she was tired of coming home to an empty apartment, which was why she rarely came home. Although her job description had stipulated that some travelling would be required, she did more than was strictly necessary.

'It's time to work on our budget,' he said. 'Do you have any suggestions?'

'Putting me on the spot?' she asked lightly.

He grinned, appearing unrepentant. 'Of course. What would you recommend?'

Warily she met his gaze. 'Honestly?'

'Honestly.'

'More staff. Two people can't handle the workload on a long-term basis, especially if you're thinking of adding more physicians. Nancy, for example, wants to start a family, but with her hours she's hardly at home. And when she is she's exhausted. You know as well as I that those are prime conditions for job burn-out. There is life outside of the hospital, you know.'

He steepled his fingers and held them to his chin, as if thinking. His brow furrowed. 'Kelly had the same complaint.'

Kelly had obviously taken advantage of the situation to cover her tracks. 'What you do with the information is, of course, up to you. But if you choose not to act on it my agency will always be available to pick up the pieces,' she finished lightheartedly.

'Vulture.' He grinned.

'Hey,' she protested, pretending affront. 'It's called a business opportunity.'

'If you say so.' He stretched out his long legs and crossed his ankles. 'By the way, you've made a good impression on a number of people.'

'We aim to please.'

'What would it take for *you* to stay?'

Her heart pounded. She'd been asked that question before and had always been able to joke her way out of a serious answer. With Andrew, however, she couldn't. His interest made it seem more personal.

'Kelly's coming. Per your request, I might add. You don't need me.'

'You just said that we're lacking in the staff department,' he reminded her.

'Yes, well…' Her mind raced after a plausible answer. Admitting that she couldn't bear to watch him resume his relationship with another woman seemed incongruous with her own hesitancy to fill the void.

'I made a fresh start two and a half years ago,' she said. 'I'm not ready to make another one.'

'You changed jobs two and a half years ago,' he corrected.

She dismissed his comment with a wave of her hand. 'Same thing.'

'Is it?'

Mariah fingered a stray thread on the hem of her shorts and blinked back the unexpected moisture forming in her eyes. He'd looked underneath and seen the stark, naked truth about her.

Her job at TLC Inc had been her saving grace, but she still clung to the remnants of her old life. Unfortunately, she didn't know how to let go. She stared at her camera case. How ironic, how sanctimonious, for her to think that a few photos would help Cal Harper accept his fate when she hadn't accepted her own. Impulsively intent on destroying her evening's work, she pulled out the first roll of film and tried to pry the metal case apart.

'What are you doing?'

'This was a mistake.' The top came off in her fumbling fingers, exposing the undeveloped film. She dug in her case for another roll. Before she could destroy it, Andrew stopped her. His large hands held hers in a steely grip.

'I can't let you do this. I won't.'

She met his gaze, her eyes swimming in tears. 'Please. My pictures won't do a thing for Cal. I shouldn't have interfered.'

Andrew tucked the film he'd confiscated into the side pocket of his jeans, then hauled her onto his lap.

'It won't do him any good,' she said, her voice catching in her throat. 'A snapshot isn't enough.'

'Of course it isn't,' he soothed, 'but it helps. You gave something to Jimmy Bleeker to hold onto while he recovered and your photos will do the same thing for Cal.'

She sniffled. 'And what do I hold onto?' She hadn't realized she'd spoken aloud until Andrew answered.

'Me,' he whispered against her hair. 'Hold onto me.'

'You seem rather mellow these days,' Nancy said a few days later as she and Mariah left the cafeteria with their lunches in hand.

'Just settling into a routine,' Mariah answered non-chalantly, hiding the real reason.

For the first time in two and a half years she felt free to enjoy a man's company on a personal level. She should have found a pair of sturdy shoulders to cry on sooner. Then again, she doubted if anyone's other than Andrew's would have yielded the same results.

Even so, she wouldn't let herself read anything more than simple friendship into his comforting arms. Dreams of a fairy-tale ending couldn't go anywhere so it was useless to pretend otherwise. In the meantime, she'd enjoy his company, and when the time came she'd leave Gallup with her heart intact.

'I thought maybe it was because you and Dr Prescott were getting along now.'

Mariah grinned. 'That, too.'

Although they'd dealt amicably with each other during the past week, they'd reached a turning point the night they'd visited Cal's home. As for the future and its associated problems, she wouldn't look further than tomorrow.

As they rounded a corner Mariah saw two boys, about six and nine years old, eyeing a vending machine. Both were scrawny and dressed in faded but clean blue jeans and T-shirts. Their reddish-brown hair, dark eyes and the smattering of freckles across their faces were too similar for them to be unrelated.

The younger one pointed to a sandwich. 'Do we have enough money?'

The older one opened his hand and counted the coins before he shook his head. 'Nope.' He squinted at the prices on display. 'Can't even buy an apple.'

'But, Darrin. I'm hungry.' The smaller one's dismay showed on his face as his anticipatory expression changed to one of utter disappointment.

Impulsively, Mariah slowed down. They reminded her of her nephews, and without an adult in sight she couldn't leave, without ensuring their welfare. 'I'll be along in a minute. Those two look like they're having a problem.'

Nancy glanced at the pair. 'You think so?' At Mariah's nod, she said, 'I'll hold down the fort. See you later.'

Mariah approached the youngsters. 'Do you need help?'

Their 'yes' and 'no' came simultaneously.

'I'm hungry,' the younger one announced, 'but Darrin don't have enough money.'

'Is your mom or dad nearby?'

'They're in the 'mergency room,' Darrin volunteered. 'Our dad hurt his shoulder.'

'I see. Does your mother know where you've gone?'

He shook his head. 'No. We're supposed to be waiting, but Derek was thirsty so we went looking for a drink.'

'And got lost,' Derek added helpfully. He studied her uniform. 'You work here?'

'Yes, I do.' She raised her serving-sized container of macaroni and cheese. 'I was about to have lunch. Would you like to join me? With your mother's permission, of course.'

Two pairs of eyes brightened and their heads bobbed up and down.

'Let's see what we can find to eat,' she said, leading the way into the cafeteria.

Darrin held out his hand to reveal two quarters and a dime. 'Will this be enough?'

A lump lodged in her throat. He sounded so hopeful that she didn't have the heart to tell him the truth. 'You bet. But, first, I'll leave a message for your parents.'

She dialled the ER from the nearest phone, having ascertained the boys' surname. 'Bonnie? I have the two Talbot boys with me in the cafeteria. Are their parents in ER?'

Bonnie's relief was palpable. 'I noticed they were missing and was just about to call for Security. Thank goodness I won't have to.'

'I'll bring them back as soon as we're finished with lunch.' Mariah replaced the receiver and turned to her young guests. 'OK, guys. Let's eat.'

After she'd surreptitiously paid the clerk, the boys wolfed down generous servings of meatloaf, mashed potatoes and green beans, as if they hadn't seen an entire meal for days.

'Do you live around Gallup?' she asked.

Darrin shook his head as he mopped up the last bit of food with a slice of bread. 'We were movin' to town, but the ranch my dad was gonna buy sold before we got here. He's gonna look for another one.'

'And what does your dad do?' she asked.

'He's a farrier. That means he shoes horses,' Derek added, his pride evident.

'There must be a lot of business around here.'

'Yup.' Derek finished his milk, then wiped away the white moustache with the back of his hand.

His brother elbowed him and the youngster obediently repeated the process with a paper napkin, before glancing at Mariah for her approval.

She smiled. 'Where will you spend the night?'

Darrin shrugged. 'My dad'll find us someplace nice. He promised.' His faith was obvious.

A vision of Cal Harper's ranch came to mind. Perhaps Cal could rest easier if he knew someone was looking after his property. She'd talk to him about it as soon as she found the chance.

'That was real good, ma'am,' Darrin said. 'We 'preciate your helpin' us.'

Derek's head bobbed in agreement.

'If you're ready, let's find your folks.' As they stepped into the elevator outside the cafeteria Derek slipped his hand into hers, before flashing her a smile.

Touched, she squeezed his hand gently in reply. A surprising new emotion tugged at her heartstrings.

Envy.

Andrew studied the radiology films, before turning to his patient, Mac Talbot. 'As I suspected, the clavicle— your collar-bone—is fractured.'

Mac nodded, wiping away the sheen of perspiration on his upper lip with short, sturdy fingers. 'I figured as much. It's happened before.'

Andrew glanced at Mac's wife, LuEllen. A red-haired woman in her early thirties, she appeared more distraught than her husband. Her lower lip quivered before she pressed her mouth into a hard line.

'According to the X-rays, you've had your share of injuries,' he commented.

'Rode bulls in my time. Broke horses to a saddle, too. Haven't met one I couldn't gentle either,' Mac boasted.

'Which is why he's in the shape he's in,' his wife blurted with exasperation.

'Now, honey, I don't do that sort of thing any more. This here was just an accident. Pure and simple. Could have happened to anyone.' He added, for Andrew's benefit, 'Tripped over my own two feet and landed against the trailer hitch.'

'The sooner we fix you up the sooner you'll feel better.' Andrew summoned Bonnie into the room to assist. After giving Mac a painkiller, he realigned the broken ends of the bone, then wrapped Mac's shoulders and upper torso in a figure-of-eight bandage, being careful to add extra padding in the area of his armpit.

Finally Bonnie adjusted Mac's sling to the right height.

'When can he go to work?' LuEllen asked.

'Several weeks, minimum.'

LuEllen's shoulders slumped.

'I also expect you to use the sling for the entire time unless you don't want the bones to heal properly. No lifting.'

Mac grimaced. 'Well, Doc, that could be a problem.'

'How so?'

'I'm a farrier by trade and I'd planned to buy a spread near here. Unfortunately, the guy I was dealing with sold the place out from under me. He gave me my down payment back, but I gotta take care of my family. I can't do that if I can't work.'

Andrew studied the couple, an idea glimmering at the back of his mind. 'I know someone who might let you rent his property, but he's eighty years old and comes with the land.'

'What do you mean?'

'He can take care of himself, but he needs someone to keep tabs on his medicine—that sort of thing. He's scheduled to enter our long-term care facility unless we can find someone to supervise him at home. Needless to say, he doesn't want to go.'

'What's he like?' LuEllen asked. 'I don't want our boys around someone who's nasty and cantankerous.'

'Cal's opinionated, but he's a nice old guy. If you're interested, I'll introduce you. If you suit each other, fine. If not, no harm done.'

The Talbots exchanged glances. 'Go ahead, Lu,' Mac said encouragingly. 'Talk to him. I trust your judgement.'

LuEllen tucked a lock of hair behind one ear. 'OK, Dr Prescott. We'll meet him.'

Andrew glanced at his watch. 'I have some paperwork to fill out, then I'll take you to his room.'

He strode into the ER hallway just as Mariah walked through the doors with two boys in tow. 'Rounding up patients?' he joked.

'Nope. Just returning some prisoners.' She ruffled Derek's hair. 'Meet Derek and Darrin Talbot. I believe their parents are here.'

Andrew nodded. 'Have a seat, boys. Your folks will be out in a minute.'

The two children complied and he lowered his voice. 'I have an idea.'

'I do, too.' Mariah grinned. 'You go first.'

Andrew tugged her away from listening ears. 'The Talbots are looking for a place to live.'

Mariah's eyes shone. 'I know. The boys told me.'

'I thought I'd ask Cal if he'd be willing to let them move in with him.'

'Perfect,' she declared in a whisper. 'I was about to make the same suggestion.'

'Great minds think alike.'

'Are they nice people?'

Andrew shrugged. 'Seem to be. I'll introduce them to

Cal as soon as I'm finished. We'll see if they take to each other.'

'I hope so.' She glanced at her watch. 'I'd love to be there, but I've left Nancy alone long enough.'

'I'll let you know what happens.'

'Today?'

He laughed at her eagerness. 'Today. I promise.'

After saying her goodbyes to the boys, she disappeared through the exit.

With her bright smile etched in his memory, Andrew hoped that she wouldn't be disappointed.

Mariah could hardly wait for the telephone to ring. Each time, however, the call concerned business rather than the situation on her mind. Her anxiety grew.

Finally, Andrew appeared in the doorway, his face impassive.

'Well?' she demanded.

His grin was slow and easy. 'It's all set. The Talbots will move in today. We'll take Cal home this weekend.'

Without thinking, she kissed him. 'Oh, Andrew. I'm so excited.'

His smile widened as he snaked his arms around her back to hold her close. 'This is a reward I hadn't expected. I could easily get used to this.'

Without a doubt, she thought. 'Was Cal hard to convince?'

'After he discovered LuEllen knew how to make pie and the boys could play checkers, he was sold on the idea. In fact, I had a hard time convincing him to wait until this weekend. I haven't seen him this perky in a long time.'

'And the Talbots?'

'Are satisfied with the arrangement.'

'I'm glad. Thank you.'

'I didn't do anything.'

'Yes, you did,' she insisted. 'If you hadn't had the same idea, you might have shot down my suggestion from the beginning, but you didn't.'

The love on his face nearly blinded her. 'Special people deserve special consideration.' He squeezed her waist. 'Much as I would like to stay, I have patients waiting in my office.'

Remembering where they were, she dropped her arms and tried to step out of his embrace. 'I'm sorry. I didn't intend to embarrass you.'

He held her firm. 'I'm not.' After giving her a swift kiss, he released her. 'Are you free this evening?'

'I'm on call.'

'Come over when you have a chance. I'll fix supper.'

'It's a date.'

The afternoon raced by. Mariah worked furiously to finish her work but her thoughts didn't stray far from his 'special people' comment. It wasn't wise to believe it pertained specifically to her, but she did.

By six o'clock she had changed her clothes and was standing on Andrew's doorstep. As soon as he'd ushered her inside, he drew her into his embrace.

'What's the occasion?' she asked, revelling in the moment.

He touched her lips. 'Just because.'

She could hardly breathe. 'The best occasion of all.'

'Interested in sightseeing? I'm going to drop by the ranch to give Clint and Karen the good news.'

'About Cal Harper?' He shook his head and she guessed again. 'Bill found the collie's owner.'

'Yes. Like we'd suspected, he'd dumped the dog but at least its vaccinations were current.' He shook his head. 'Why the man didn't take the dog to a humane society, I'll never know. In any case, Chester is ecstatic.'

'I'll bet.'

'While we're at the ranch, I'll show you the pond. You might want to take a few pictures. Afterwards, we can rent a movie.'

'I'd like that.' Her obligations came to mind. 'What if the hospital needs me?'

'It's only five miles from town. I can have you back in a few minutes.' He drew away somewhat reluctantly. 'I'd better check the grill. Make yourself at home.'

Mariah wandered across the entryway and into the living room. His furniture consisted of a hodgepodge of antiques, all lovingly cared for. The only contemporary piece was his sofa.

His love for old-fashioned things carried into the combination kitchen and dining room. A well-preserved pie safe and an impressively carved oak table with a matching china cupboard caught her eye. His decorating taste leaned to earth tones—shades of brown, green and an occasional burgundy for a splash of colour. The house was homey and she liked it.

He walked inside, smelling of wood-smoke and barbecue sauce. 'Hope you like chicken.'

'I love it.' She pointed to the bare walls, imagining how perfect several of her photographs would look there. 'How long have you lived here?'

He thought a moment. 'About a year. Want to see the rest of it?'

'Could I?'

'Sure.' He led her down a hallway and flung open a door. 'This is the master bedroom. It has its own bath.' The room was neat and decorated in the same colour scheme as the rest of his house.

Her gaze landed on the king-sized bed. 'Nice,' she said. His presence emphasized the room's purpose and a shiver ran through her, turning her insides to molten lava.

'Here's my office.' He led her to the next door, then stepped aside to allow her entrance. 'The desk was my grandfather's.'

She ran her hand over the roll-top desk, catching the faint scent of lemon oil. 'It's beautiful.' Unlike the walls in the other room, this one displayed his diplomas and an oil painting of a clipper, sailing stormy seas.

'And this one…' he pointed across the hallway '…is a spare bedroom.'

She peered inside, surprised to see a wallpaper border with animals in a Noah's ark motif. A twin bed stood in a corner, along with a dresser.

The significance of the room caught her. 'This must be…'

He shrugged, clearly sheepish. 'Kelly chose the decor while we were building. After she left I forgot about the paper she'd ordered. By the time I remembered, the contractor had already hung it. My nephew calls it his room.'

Mariah surveyed the pattern. It was perfect for a child. Suddenly, Kelly's deception weighed heavily on her mind. Once Kelly returned, Andrew would want Carlie to occupy the room her mother had designed.

After all, Kelly would be here and Mariah wouldn't. The adage, 'out of sight, out of mind,' would apply.

She couldn't bear to think about it. The prospect was simply too painful.

'What do you think?' he asked.

Mariah cleared her throat to gain time. 'It's gorgeous.'

Hiding her anguish, she asked brightly, 'Is there anything I can do to help you with dinner?'

'Not a thing. I'll take the salad out of the refrigerator. Our kebabs should be finished by now.'

He headed down the hallway to the patio, leaving her to stare at Noah's animals. She wouldn't think about the future, she told herself. For now she'd concentrate on the few weeks she had left and enjoy every minute of her time with Andrew. She had no right to feel jealous. She wasn't ready for an intense relationship with anyone.

Take each day as it comes, she said in her mind. Becky had planted one bulb at a time, and Mariah would live one moment at a time. It would have to be enough.

Two hours later Mariah stared across the pasture. The Hereford cattle in the lush grass, the family of ducks on the surface of Andrew's pond and the patch of wildflowers, swaying in the gentle breeze, made her finger itch to snap the camera shutter.

'This is beautiful. So peaceful.' She focused her telephoto lens on the ducks for a close-up shot.

He grinned his lazy grin and leaned against his Land Cruiser's front grill. 'I agree. I'm glad you like it.'

She pointed to the water. 'Do you fish?'

'Not lately,' he said with regret. 'The days don't seem to have enough hours.' He straightened. 'Come on. I'll show you where I fell out of the tree and broke my arm.'

'Marked the spot, did you?'

'Of course. That was a memorable moment in my life.'

Mariah imagined a younger version of the virile man in front of her. 'I'll bet.'

The grass swished against their shoes as they walked

the short distance. Standing under the tree, Andrew pointed to a branch several feet above his head. 'That's the one.'

She shielded her eyes from the sun and peeked through the leaves. 'Goodness, you could have been killed.'

'I realize that now, but at the time I was only interested in impressing Kelly. She'd shinnied up to the same branch so I couldn't let myself be outdone. Not by a mere *girl*, anyway.'

She rested one hand against the trunk. Her fingertips encountered a rough spot and she leaned closer to look. Someone had crudely carved a heart into the bark with the initials 'A' and 'K' inside.

The sight sent an odd jolt through her. 'Your handiwork?'

'What cub scout with a new pocketknife could resist?'

She traced the 'A'. 'You spent a lot of time here, didn't you?'

'Yes. I loved every minute of it, too.' He gazed across the field. 'I'm thinking about selling it.'

'You're what?'

'Clint's wanted to buy it for a long time.'

'You're not willing to hang onto it? Like Cal?' The idea was inconceivable. Andrew fitted into the scenery too well to deny his heritage.

He bent to snatch up a blade of grass. 'Cal's home is a symbol of his independence. He doesn't want to relinquish it. I, on the other hand, don't face the same problem.'

'But it's a part of you. Don't you want to share it with your—' her voice cracked '—children?'

'We can always visit.'

'But I thought you loved the land.'

'I do. So does Clint. In fact, it's more his than mine because he's a rancher at heart.'

'And you're not.'

He hesitated. 'Medicine is more interesting to me and I'm not embarrassed to admit it. Even so, I wouldn't consider selling to anyone but Clint. I can let go of the land, knowing it's in good hands.' Straightening, he reached for her hand. 'Enough serious talk. Let's take some pictures.'

She grinned. 'You got it.'

Over the next hour she tramped through the meadow, snapping pictures of flowers, ducks and the oak tree. At various times she focused on Andrew, capturing his tousled hair and special grin. As she panned the scene to take the final pictures of her roll, she focused on Andrew, staring into the distance. Silhouetted against the lowering sun, with one foot propped on a large rock, he appeared like a man at peace with himself and his world. But as she zoomed in on his face she saw more than that. She saw his strength of character, his loyalty, his integrity and even a glimmer of longing on his features.

This was a man she could easily fall in love with, if she could only take the final, irrevocable step. Fear held her back, fear of losing him in one form or another.

She snapped the shutter several times in succession, knowing these shots would be some of her best. Without seeing the final product, she imagined how she'd display them. She'd make a collage, using a simple frame of weathered wood to bring out the background. It would be one of her treasured possessions.

The whirring noise of the film automatically rewinding disrupted nature's peace. Andrew straightened from his casual pose. 'All finished?'

'Yes. I'm anxious to see how they turn out.'

Andrew slung his arm around her waist as they

walked toward his vehicle, releasing her only long enough to slide behind the wheel. Once inside, he patted the seat next to him.

She didn't need a second invitation. Nestling against him for the return trip, she revelled in the feel of his arm around her and the hard length of his thigh against hers.

Closing her eyes, she let her thoughts drift as the radio whispered a slow country song in the background and Andrew's tangy scent surrounded her.

'You make a good assistant photographer,' she said, her voice husky.

He squeezed her closer. 'It's all in the hands.'

Her mind flashed back to other photo sessions. Dave had talked non-stop, always pointing out the things he'd thought she'd missed. In contrast, Andrew hovered in the background, maintaining a low profile.

'No,' she insisted, 'it's more than that. You understand there's a certain concentration to the work—figuring out the best lighting, the best angle—to capture the moment. So many people think I just snap pictures mindlessly.'

He flashed her a grin. 'Thanks for the compliment. Does this mean you'll take me with you again?'

'I'll take you any time.'

In that instant she realized something monumental. She'd thought of Dave and the memory hadn't left the usual feeling of guilt in its wake. Nor had the quicksand of despair pulled her into its grip.

She didn't know if she should laugh or cry. She wanted to do both. In the distance she saw the city's lights, and a few minutes later Andrew parked in front of her house.

She smiled up at him. 'Ready for that movie?'

He unwound his arm from her shoulders and leaned against his door. 'No.'

His eyes were intent, telegraphing his unspoken question eloquently. She cleared her throat but her voice still sounded husky. 'Then what do you want to do?'

'Do you have to ask?'

His meaning was obvious. She knew why he'd moved away fractionally. He was giving her a moment to decide, a moment for her head to make the decision without her body's interference.

'I'm flattered,' she began slowly. 'I really am. But—'

'You're not ready. I know.'

Puzzled, she touched his denim-clad thigh. 'What makes you say that?'

Andrew reached for her hand. Her *left* hand. 'This.'

She stared at her engagement ring, unable to answer. Such a small thing, but with huge significance. She lifted her gaze to his, certain her eyes reflected her inner turmoil.

'When we make love I don't want anyone else in that bed except you and me.'

Tears came to her eyes. 'Oh, Andrew.' Her hands dropped to her lap. She didn't know what to say.

'In any case,' he continued, 'I didn't say all this to force you into anything. I mentioned it because I thought you should know the direction I'm headed.'

'Where you're headed?' she said lamely.

Andrew caressed her cheek. 'I want more than the next few weeks, Mariah. I'm talking years. A lifetime. I'm here for you. Waiting.'

She buried her nose against his shirt. She wanted to, she really did. But would Andrew make the same offer once Kelly reappeared on the scene?

CHAPTER EIGHT

OVER the next week Mariah began to feel as if she were on the brink of a change. After several evenings, spent in Andrew's company, she realized how much she'd insulated herself from the world. Her work had become her cocoon and she'd woven it tightly around herself. If, prior to this, someone had accused her of being stifled, she would have dismissed it as pure nonsense.

Thanks to Andrew, she now saw her life in a different light. Something inside urged her to break out of the protective shell and try her proverbial wings. For her to contemplate such a move suggested that the time for action was near.

Pushing off with her foot, she sent the porch swing into motion, unable to keep Andrew out of her thoughts as she waited for him to arrive. She loved being in his company. He was authoritative—a man of action—but not domineering. Her opinions were as important as his and he always listened to her suggestions. Just the other day Nancy had informed her of the budget committee's authorization to add two new lab positions, based on Andrew's recommendations.

She'd planned to tamp down her attraction to him, but her intentions were becoming harder and harder to obey. Perhaps she was wrong to spend her free time with him but, technically, there was no reason why she couldn't. Like her, he wasn't married or engaged, although on an emotional level the situation wasn't as clear-cut. Taking each day as it came had served her well before. It would in this instance also.

Becky rounded the corner of the house and bounded up the steps. 'I thought I'd find you here.'

'I'm becoming a creature of habit, aren't I?'

Becky sat on one of the deck chairs. 'It's too nice to be indoors so I don't blame you.' She motioned across the street. 'Nice view, too.'

Mariah's face warmed. 'Andrew has a lovely home.'

'He does,' Becky agreed. 'It's a shame he spends most of his time at the hospital and his office, although lately I've noticed he's in the neighbourhood more often.'

'Is he?'

'Definitely. I'm not the only one who's noticed,' Becky said. 'Anything that concerns Drew Prescott concerns nearly everyone in town.'

'One of the dubious perks of small-town living.' Mariah said, a wry note to her voice.

'Speaking of small-town living, is there a chance you'll move to Gallup?'

Mariah shrugged. 'I can't say. It depends on a lot of things. My job for one. I've been promoted to a vice-presidential position.'

'Impressive.'

She laughed. 'Simply put, I'm being placed in charge of expanding the scope of TLC Inc. Not only do we want to provide temporary help to medical facilities, we want to add a job placement branch. I'm excited about the idea.'

Becky pressed her lips into a line and a wrinkle appeared on her forehead. 'And what about Andrew?'

Mariah drew a deep breath and stared into the distance. How could she admit that her future depended upon the plans of two other people? 'I can't make any decisions until I'm sure of what I want and what Andrew wants.'

'There's no doubt in my mind of what Andrew wants,' Becky declared. 'I've seen the way he looks at you. He's biding his time, but with the right encouragement the man would lose control. You'd have the night of your life.'

'Becky!' Instant heat flooded Mariah's face and she rocked the swing faster to cool her skin.

'Don't be embarrassed,' Becky said kindly. 'As for knowing what you want, I understand your caution. I've started seeing someone, too.'

Mariah stopped swinging. 'Really?'

Becky nodded. 'We've had a few dates. Loren's a nice man. Given time, we'll get around to a physical relationship.' She grinned. 'There's a lot to be said for anticipation.'

Thinking of Andrew's embraces—the quivery sensation his touch created in her body—Mariah agreed.

'If you're like me, and I suspect you are to a certain degree, you've felt guilty about your feelings for Andrew.'

Mariah nodded. 'And then I'd feel guilty for feeling guilty. Everyone told me to move on with my life because Dave was gone, that he wouldn't expect me to be alone. In my head I knew it was true, but my heart wasn't willing. I think I'm past that now, but—'

'You're not ready for the next level.' Becky sighed. 'It isn't easy to take that step.'

'No, it isn't,' Mariah whispered.

'Don't worry. When the conditions are right you'll know in here.' Becky tapped her chest. 'A wise woman told me that a long time ago. I didn't believe her at first, but now I do.'

'Who is she? Your mother?'

'Actually, my aunt. I assume she knows what she's talking about as she's buried two husbands and is working on her third.'

Mariah couldn't resist. 'Burying him?'

Becky laughed. 'Finding him.' She eyed the package on Mariah's lap. 'What's on tap for this evening? Not working on your other job's paperwork again, I hope.'

With the mood lightened, Mariah relaxed. 'No. Andrew and I are going to visit Cal Harper and the Talbots.' She lifted the sturdy envelope. 'My neighbour in Denver has her own darkroom so she develops my photographs. I hope they came out.'

Becky slid to the edge of her chair. 'May I see?'

'If you'd like.' Mariah ripped into the protective cardboard sleeve and pulled out a large brown envelope. She read the yellow sticky note on the outside and grinned.

Glad to see you're back in the saddle. I took the liberty of enlarging them, especially the one of the handsome dude. I'm expecting all the details when you return.

'All' had been underlined three times.

She reached inside the second envelope and pulled out a handful of 8×10 inch photographs. The one on top showed Sniffles, snuggled against little Jimmy Bleeker. The puppy rested its head on Jimmy's chest and stared with soulful eyes at his young master.

Becky stood to peer over Mariah's shoulder. 'My goodness. The dog looks positively worried.'

Satisfaction filled Mariah's being. She handed it to Becky. 'It turned out well. Jimmy will enjoy knowing Sniffles was as concerned for him as he was for Sniffles.'

The picture of Becky's house, surrounded by a yellow carpet of daffodils, sent Becky into shocked surprise. 'How beautiful! When did you do this?'

'About a week ago. Would you like to keep it?'

'Would I? Do you have to ask?'

'Then it's yours. With my best wishes.'

'Really?'

Mariah smiled. 'Yes, really.' Cal's homestead photographs came next. Gazing at the pictures, she could almost feel the breeze turning the windmill, touch the oak leaves, hear the creak of the weathered pine steps.

'You're wasting your talent,' Becky declared.

'If Cal and Jimmy like them, my talents aren't wasted.' She moved to the next photo and her breath caught in her throat. Andrew's likeness stared back at her with enough clarity for her to relive every moment of their memorable evening.

'What's wrong?' Becky peered down at the enlargement. 'Oh my.'

For a few minutes neither spoke. Mariah had caught Andrew in a pensive mood. His strength of character showed in the angles of his face and in his solid stance as he stared into the distance, thinking thoughts so private they couldn't be voiced.

She'd captured an unforgettable glimpse of a truly unforgettable person. A knot formed at the back of her throat and her heart swelled in her chest.

'You love him, don't you?' Becky's voice was soft.

Mariah stared at his image and her mouth curved into a faint smile. 'Yes.' Heaven help her.

Becky hugged her. 'I'm so happy for you. I hope you have a long life together.'

If only it were possible, thought Mariah. She wanted to believe in a happy ending, but happy endings were elusive. Remembering his affirmation to help Kelly with her problems, she didn't need a crystal ball to visualize the scene or predict the outcome once Kelly pulled into town.

Just then Andrew drove up. He stuck his arm through the open window and waved.

'Please don't tell anyone,' Mariah begged, watching him step out of the vehicle and advance toward them.

Becky patted her shoulder. 'Say no more. My lips are sealed. Why don't you run in and freshen up? I'll keep him occupied.'

Mariah gratefully fled inside, taking the photograph of Andrew with her. Through the open window she could hear their voices but not the conversation. No matter, her mind was on more important things than their casual chat.

Perhaps she should seize the moment—gamble for once in her life. A few short weeks of bliss would be better than nothing. Wouldn't it?

She hurried into the bedroom, twisting her ring as she tried to visualize Dave's face. To her dismay, his features had blurred and, try as she might, she couldn't bring them into focus. Sinking onto the coverlet her grandmother had hand-quilted, she reached for the engagement photo beside her bed and outlined Dave's likeness.

He seemed like a stranger. She couldn't recall his scent, his mannerisms or his touch in vivid detail any longer—only a general impression remained. Instead, Andrew's traits had taken root in her memory.

'Goodbye,' she said, as Dave's image swam through her unshed tears. 'I loved every moment we were together, but I have to move on with my life. Don't worry, though. I won't forget you. You'll always hold a special corner in my heart.'

A tear streaked down her face and she swiped it away. Gathering her courage, she placed the frame face down in the bedside table's drawer. Knowing what she was about to do was emotionally irrevocable, she drew a deep breath and tugged off the ring Dave had placed on her finger.

She crossed the small room to her jewellery box and slid the band into a padded slot. As she closed the lid she closed a chapter in her life as well.

Her hand felt bare. Fear of the unknown reared its ugly head, but she tamped down the feeling. She only had one direction to go. Forward.

'What are you doing tonight?' Becky asked brightly.

Andrew's eyes narrowed. 'What's going on?'

'What do you mean?'

'You've asked me that question three times in the last ten minutes. Also, you can't seem to sit still.'

Becky waved her hand to chase away an irritating fly. 'I'm old and forgetful. My joints are stiff.'

'You're only forty-eight. That's not old. You also have a memory like a steel trap and spend every morning doing step aerobics. Try another story.'

She leaned closer. 'We had a rather enlightening talk while we were waiting for you. Mariah needs a few minutes alone.'

An enlightening talk? He glared at her. 'What did you discuss?'

'Lots of things—her job at TLC, Dave, you.' She lowered her voice. 'Out of curiosity, and you can tell me to mind my own business, but how *do* you feel about Kelly coming home?'

'I'm happy for her parents, especially her mother. As for myself...' he shrugged '...it will be nice to see an old friend again. Unfortunately, I don't think Mariah believes me.'

Becky studied him with a troubled gaze. 'I understand why she wouldn't. You haven't seen Kelly in over a year. Might be some long-forgotten embers get stirred when you do, leaving Mariah on the outside. Naturally she's leery of getting her heart trampled in the process.'

He shook his head. 'Not a chance.'

As if satisfied with his response, Becky handed Mariah's envelope to Andrew. 'By the way, you must see her pictures. I'm sure she won't mind.'

He studied each one, hardly able to believe his eyes. Although Mariah had depicted common scenes, she had managed to portray an emotional element as well. 'Look beyond the surface,' she'd once said. She was obviously a master at it.

'She's a rare woman, isn't she?' Becky asked. 'A pearl of great price. You'd better hang onto her.'

He grinned. 'I'll do my best.'

The screen door opened and Mariah stepped outside. 'Do your best at what?'

Andrew exchanged a glance with Becky. 'To keep our visit with Cal short so he can get to bed early.'

'Oh.' She smiled a twenty-four carat smile. 'I'm ready if you are.'

'Sorry I'm late. I had an unexpected patient walk in at the last minute—one of my asthma patients has bronchitis.'

'No problem.'

Andrew guided Mariah down the steps with his hand at the small of her back. Her hair smelled of apples—

delicious, edible apples. 'See you later, Beck,' he called over his shoulder.

'Have a nice time.'

Feeling naked without her ring, Mariah was certain the white area on her finger gleamed like a neon sign. She kept her hands in her pockets, unwilling to advertise her recent change of heart.

Andrew ushered her toward his Toyota. 'I hope you're hungry because I certainly am.'

'I've waited all day for this,' she confessed. 'Next time I'll fix something for you. That is, if I can find a cookbook.'

'You can't cook?'

'I can, but I haven't for a long time. Being on the road, it's impossible, and when I'm at home it isn't worth the effort. But I'm willing to try again, provided you're equally willing to be my guinea pig.'

He grinned. 'I'd be honoured. But, if something happens to me, make sure you have them put a catchy phrase on my tombstone.'

'Something like, ''He died with his boots under my table''?' she asked, altering another western expression.

'Yeah, but something snappier.'

'I'll work on it,' she said wryly.

After a meal at Chester's restaurant they headed out of town. As Andrew turned into Cal's drive Mariah braced herself for a bumpy ride. To her surprise, someone had filled in the potholes and erased the washboard ridges.

'Looks like the Talbots have been hard at work,' she commented.

'I hope Mac hasn't done it,' he said. 'His shoulder can't stand the strain.'

When they drove into the yard she noticed more

changes. The drunken shutters were fixed in precise rows, the broken window panes replaced and the scraggly-looking yard mowed.

Mariah hopped out to survey the improvements, hearing the sound of childish laughter echo across the clearing. She closed her eyes for a second and took a deep breath. 'This place has come alive. Can you feel it?'

Andrew nodded. 'Absolutely. It's remarkable.'

Cal rose out of his chair on the porch and waved. 'About time you got here. We've been savin' dessert. The boys could hardly wait.'

'Where are they?' Mariah asked, certain it was more a case of Cal's wishes than the boys'.

'Explorin' in the barn. Those kids don't stop from mornin' until night. Just watchin' 'em plum wears me out, but it's good havin' 'em around.' Cal stared across his land. 'Makes me feel younger.'

LuEllen came out of the house and Mac followed. 'Cal, you should have told us that your company got here.'

'We just drove in,' Andrew assured her.

Mariah glanced around. 'You've been working hard.'

Mac grinned. 'Yup. But I can't take the credit. Cal, LuEllen and the boys have done the most.' He patted his arm, still in its sling. 'I just supervise.'

'It's gratifying to hear someone has actually followed my orders,' Andrew said. He turned to Cal. 'Any problems I should know about?'

Cal shook his head. 'Not a one. LuEllen keeps track of my pills like clockwork. It's awful nice not to worry about takin' 'em. Don't know what I'd do without her.'

'He's doing well,' LuEllen interjected, her face colouring under Cal's praise. 'The home health nurse still stops by, but she's cut her visits down to twice a week.'

'Enough about me. How about some pie?' Cal leaned closer. 'LuEllen makes the best cherry pie I ever tasted.'

'I'd love some,' Mariah said.

'Make yourself at home,' LuEllen said. 'I'll be right out. Mac, fetch the boys, please?'

By the time Mac returned from his errand she'd reappeared in the doorway, carrying a large tray with saucers, silverware and the coveted dessert.

'The boys will be here in a minute,' Mac said.

As Cal had predicted, the pie was the best Mariah had ever eaten. 'This is wonderful,' she said enthusiastically. 'You ought to sell these. You'd make a fortune.'

'Thank you.' Once again LuEllen blushed a becoming shade of pink.

Her husband hugged her with his good arm. 'That's what I've been telling her, but she wouldn't believe me.'

Without warning, a scream of pain rent the peaceful atmosphere. Forks stopped in mid-air and panic arose on the Talbots' faces.

'It's Derek.' LuEllen dropped her saucer and rushed down the steps, two strides behind Andrew and Mac.

Cal's face turned pasty white. Mariah hated to leave the elderly man alone as Derek would receive plenty of attention. She moved to the chair beside him and held his hand.

'He'll be fine,' she said encouragingly.

Cal shook his head. 'I hope so. There's a lot of old stuff in there that could hurt a young un real bad.'

'Then it's a lucky thing Andrew was here.'

Darrin raced out of the barn and into the house. 'Golly. He's bleeding all over the place.' The door slammed behind him and reopened a few seconds later. He flew over the threshold and ran toward the barn, with a white teatowel fluttering like a flag behind him.

'Go check on him, then come an' tell me,' Cal ordered. 'I'll be fine. I won't have a heart attack or nothin' while I'm waitin', but the suspense is killin' me.'

Mariah didn't need a second urging. She paused on the threshold for her eyes to adjust to the dim light before she proceeded inside the dusty barn. Making her way towards the group surrounding the boy on the ground, she breathed in the familiar scent of hay and animals. 'How is he?'

'He fell off the ladder, leading to the loft. Somehow he ended up with a nail in his foot and a gash to his left arm,' Andrew reported.

The towel wrapped around Derek's arm was stained red. He lay on the ground, his foot propped on Andrew's knee. A wooden board was attached to the sole of his sneaker.

'Come on, buddy. Let's get you where we can see the damage better.' Andrew lifted the child in his arms and carried him to the porch, where he conducted his examination under several pairs of watchful eyes.

'He'll need stitches in his arm. How long has it been since his last tetanus vaccination?'

'When he had his DPT series as a baby,' LuEllen replied.

'Do you have any antiseptic and bandages?' At LuEllen's nod, Andrew continued, 'Get them. We'll pull the nail out and clean his foot.'

'No-o-o,' Derek cried.

'It'll be over before you know it,' Andrew promised. As soon as LuEllen returned, he grabbed the board near the point of attachment. 'Now, Derek, I want you to—' He pulled the wood free. 'Relax. It's over.'

'It's over?'

'You bet.' Andrew untied Derek's laces and slipped

the shoe and sock off his foot. A small puncture wound in the boy's heel bled freely. 'This may sting while I clean it out. Luckily you were wearing your shoes. The nail didn't go in as deep as it could have.'

Mariah stared at the board, noticing its offending two-inch spike had only its tip bloodied.

Andrew taped the bandage over Derek's heel. 'One wound down. One to go.'

Darrin poked his head over Mariah's shoulder to observe the proceedings. 'How many stitches is he gonna need?'

'Fifteen or so.'

Darrin's eyes widened and an envious expression crossed his face. 'Wow. The most I've had is six.'

Derek's shoulders straightened with pride. 'Can I have a sling like my dad?'

'We'll work something out.' Andrew ruffled the boy's hair. 'After we're finished, though, you won't be able to get your arm wet.'

'Did you hear that, Mom? No baths.'

Andrew laughed and Mariah smiled at his obvious excitement. 'Sorry, son. I'm sure your mom will work something out.'

Mariah glanced at Cal. His expression had gone from worried to tired. 'He's going to be fine,' she said softly, pleased to see Cal's nod in response.

'It's a good thing this happened to my left arm,' Derek said.

'Why's that?' his mother asked.

He held up his right hand. ''Cause this is my checker hand. I can keep Cal comp'ny while I'm recupering.'

Cal's tension appeared to ease and he managed a toothy smile.

'I think you mean "recuperating",' LuEllen corrected him.

'Whatever.'

Andrew rose. 'If you want to bring him in your truck, Mariah and I will meet you in the ER.'

LuEllen shot an uneasy glance at her husband. 'We shouldn't leave Darrin...'

'Don't be ridiculous,' Cal snapped. 'The boy and I'll be fine until you get back. Won't we?'

Darrin nodded.

'Then it's settled,' Andrew said. 'We'll see you at the hospital.'

A short time later Mariah stood in the ER nurses' station, waiting for Andrew to suture Derek's arm. In less than an hour the Talbots were on their way home.

'Going out with you is always exciting,' Mariah teased, as he finished his paperwork in the exam room. She was acutely aware that the night was still relatively young, and she didn't want to waste the time, watching television or stargazing. Having been out of circulation for so long, she was nervous about how to proceed and so she hid her jitters behind humour. 'I wonder what sort of medical emergency we'll run into next time.'

He balanced the clipboard on the small sink, before advancing toward her. 'I foresee a case requiring mouth-to-mouth resuscitation.'

She stepped into his embrace. 'You do?'

He lowered his head until their lips were barely touching. 'Yes.'

'Who's the patient?' she whispered.

'I am.' He pressed his mouth against hers. She tasted the sweetness of cherries, and smelt the same fragrance on his breath.

'I'd be happy to lend aid, but I'd rather do it at home,' she said in a come-hither voice.

He stilled. Lifting his head, he gazed down at her, his face wreathed in shadows. 'Are you sure? I won't come in unless I'll be there for breakfast.'

This was her opening. No matter what the future held, she intended to make the most of this opportunity. 'How do you like your toast?' she asked.

'Buttered. Jelly, if you have it.'

'It's a deal.'

'My place or yours?'

'Mine.' She could have chosen Andrew's but she wanted him in *her* bed.

'You're sure?' he repeated in a whisper.

'With my whole heart.'

He needed no further urging. Grabbing the clipboard in one hand, he flung open the door and nearly ploughed into Bonnie.

'I'd hoped you hadn't left—' the nurse began. Her expression brought trepidation to Mariah's heart.

'What's wrong?' Andrew asked.

'Gary Wright's wife, Tricia, just called. She thinks Gary's having a heart attack.'

CHAPTER NINE

ANDREW took a second to recover from the shock. 'Did Tricia give you any information?'

Bonnie shook her head. 'She said she's bringing Gary in because he's having a heart attack. I didn't have a chance to ask any questions because she hung up right away.'

Andrew grimaced. He'd been encouraging Gary to lose those thirty or so pounds that had crept on his frame. He'd hoped his friend hadn't started with a strenuous exercise programme.

The automatic doors whooshed open and Tricia rushed in, holding Gary's arm as if she expected him to collapse.

Bonnie rushed forward with a wheelchair. 'Have a seat, Gary.' At the mulish set to his face, she chided him. 'You're not an employee now—you're a patient. The rules say you ride so don't argue.'

He plonked himself into the seat, muttering under his breath. A moment later Bonnie whisked him into the trauma room.

Andrew glanced at Mariah, mentally telegraphing his sorrow at the interruption. She smiled in response. 'I'll wait in the nurses' station.'

'Thanks.' He turned on his heel in search of his patient. By the time he entered the trauma room Gary was resting on the gurney, which had been adjusted to a sitting position.

'Would you stop hovering?' Gary told his wife

crossly. 'I don't know why I let you talk me into this. Andrew, would you explain to her about the difference between heartburn and a heart attack?'

'I know the difference,' Tricia snapped. 'Heartburn doesn't cause sweating, a pain in your arm or nausea.'

Gary rolled his eyes. 'She bought one of those family medical guides and now she thinks she's a doctor.'

Tricia faced Andrew. 'I just want him checked out.'

'I will.' Andrew studied Gary, noting his flushed face and a sheen of perspiration dotting his upper lip. 'So your arm hurts?'

'Yeah. I've been playing tennis which is why I'm sweaty. Stretched too far on a swing and pulled a muscle.'

'How do you feel otherwise?'

'Lousy. I've got this pain here that won't stop.' He pointed to the upper left quadrant of his abdomen. 'I've been taking antacids and they usually help, but not tonight.'

'You might have an ulcer,' Andrew commented. 'Since you're here, we'll check everything out. Blood work, X-rays, EKG—the works.'

Gary rolled his eyes, appearing resigned. Andrew motioned to Bonnie as he began to listen to Gary's heart. 'Send Mariah in. Call the EKG tech, too.'

Mariah sat in the nurses' station, drumming her fingers on the counter as she waited for the inevitable summons. When Bonnie came into the hallway and crooked her finger, Mariah jumped to her feet. Cardiac work-ups would take at least an hour and she was eager to start.

As soon as she entered the trauma room Andrew spoke. 'Run a cardiac profile, electrolytes, BUN and an amylase to rule out pancreatitis. If the CK is elevated, I'll want the MB fraction as well.'

She nodded. The heart was rich in creatine kinase enzyme and any damage caused an elevation in the total CK activity and the myocardial or MB component as well.

After taking her supplies from the lab's emergency cache, she approached Gary with tubes in hand while Andrew retreated to the foot of the gurney. 'You know what I want,' she said with a smile.

'Afraid so.' He glared at his wife, who was clearly undaunted by his criticisms. 'Man, I hate needles.'

'So do I,' Mariah said. 'Which is why I always make sure I'm on this side of them.'

He managed a grin. Just as Mariah inserted the point under his skin Gary clutched his chest and gasped.

'Andrew!' Mariah called, but her cry was unnecessary. Andrew moved to Gary's side in the blink of an eye. 'Get me those results stat. Where's the EKG tech?'

Bonnie hurriedly lowered the head of the gurney as Andrew began barking out orders. The atmosphere was transformed from calm to frantic and the small room instantly became a hive of activity.

Mariah rushed through the halls at a fast clip. The sooner Andrew had those results the better.

The loudspeaker broke the silence. 'Code Blue. ER. Code Blue. ER.'

The message spurred her on as she sent up a silent prayer for Gary, for Andrew and for Gary's wife. She whizzed around the lab, bent on speed. Little by little she collected data, most of it normal. At long last the chemistry analyzer spat out a section of printer paper. The CK was elevated to nearly three times normal.

She called the result to the woman who answered the ER phone, promising the CK-MB figure in minutes. As she'd suspected, that result was also high, indicating damage to the heart muscle some time during the past six hours. Tricia had done the right thing by bringing Gary to the hospital.

After calling the final results to ER, she tidied the department and readied her equipment for the next case. Eager to hear what was happening, she rushed back to ER and found Bonnie, scurrying through the hallway.

'How's Gary?'

'We're transferring him to Casper. The air ambulance should be here any minute.'

'I'm glad.'

'I hope he makes it to their cardiac care unit. He's been hard to stabilize.'

A sympathetic pain stabbed Mariah's heart. 'His wife?'

'She's with Andrew.' Bonnie wiped her eyes. 'I feel so badly for her. She has two kids to look after and no other family around.'

The sound of a woman weeping caught Mariah's attention. She turned to see Andrew leading Tricia from the trauma room, his arms around her as her shoulders shook with sobs.

The situation hit too close to home. An urge to escape came over her. 'I'll be around if you need me,' Mariah said, before she fled the ER.

Outside the building she slowed to a walk. Tears ran down her face as she relived those moments when Dave's doctor had broken the news.

For Tricia's sake, she hoped the woman wouldn't experience the same anguish. Mariah understood how difficult it was to pick up the broken threads and weave them into another life. She prayed the woman and her two children wouldn't be forced to look back on the plans they'd made for their family and see how they'd been erased.

The sound of an approaching helicopter and the blinking lights caught her attention as it landed. In less time than she'd thought possible, it flew into the night in the direction from which it had come.

Her work over, she went home. As she tucked her feet underneath her while she sat on the sofa in her dimly lit living room, her energy deserted her. Leaning against the cushions, she slipped into a doze.

At three a.m. a noise roused her. She clicked on the porch light and saw Andrew outside the door. His hair was dishevelled and his face appeared haggard. Without a word, she welcomed him inside.

'How is he?'

'Stable for the moment.'

Relief ran through and her shoulders slumped. 'I'm glad. Seeing him when he first came into ER, I never dreamed anything was seriously wrong.'

'Neither did he. He owes his life to Tricia and her home medical guide.' His watch beeped the hour. 'I should go. I didn't realize it was so late, but I thought you'd want to hear.'

'Please stay. I need you.' Her smile was shaky.

His eyes searched hers. 'You're sure?'

Mariah placed her left hand in his. 'I'm positive. Gary and Tricia got their happy ending, more or less. I want mine, at least for tonight.'

He glanced down. A slow, appreciative grin spread across his face as he clearly understood the significance of her bare finger. Immediately his mouth came down on hers. His fingers travelled along the curve of her breast, sending a shower of delightful shivers along her spine.

Mariah heard a rasp of zippers and her shirt disappeared, allowing the air to caress her overheated skin. Her fingers wrestled with Andrew's buttons until finally they walked across the light dusting of hair on his chest. His heart beat under her hand and she couldn't stop her groan of anticipation.

For a few hours she intended to reaffirm life and not death, to wish for and believe in happy endings.

The alarm shrilled at six a.m. Sighing at the intrusion, Mariah reached out to silence the noise. The morning air seemed especially cool after sleeping against Andrew's warm body, and she gratefully returned to snuggling against his side.

'What time is it?' he asked, his voice husky.

'Six.'

He rubbed his eyes. 'It's Saturday.'

'It's also my weekend to work,' Mariah reminded as she ran her hand across his ribs.

He rose on one elbow to stare at her as he lowered the percale bedsheet a few inches to trace the upper curve of her breast. 'Darn. I had other plans for the weekend.'

'I did, too,' she said with remorse, feeling her body's response to his light hand.

'What time will you be home?'

She thought for a moment. 'With luck, around three.'

'That's a long time to wait.'

His mournful expression made her laugh. 'Ah, but by then we'll both be tired and ready for a relaxing afternoon.' She stroked his stubbly face. 'Also, you'll have shaved.'

Andrew looked sheepish. 'I'd forgotten. Can't have

you going to work with whisker burn on your face.' His expression brightened. 'There are other—'

She giggled, feeling like a schoolgirl. 'I'd love to, but if I'm late getting to the lab I'll play catch-up for the rest of the day. I won't mention any names,' she said with mock seriousness, 'but there are certain doctors who become rather testy when they're making rounds and lab results aren't waiting on the chart.'

'Spoilsport,' he grumbled good-naturedly.

'I know. But I'm off next weekend.'

His eyes brightened. 'Keep it open,' he ordered. 'I plan to fill it.'

'It's a deal.' Mariah sat up, wondering how to make a graceful exit without a robe. Morning-after protocol hadn't been considered when she'd invited him in early this morning.

Andrew reached down to pick his shirt off the floor. 'Want this?'

She grabbed it. 'Thanks.' Presenting her back to him, she let the sheet fall, before sliding her arms through the sleeves. The fabric retained his scent and she inhaled deeply as she buttoned it.

'Ready for breakfast?' she asked, rising.

'Yeah, but I'll make it while you're getting ready.' He hopped out of bed and pulled on his jeans, leaving the top snap undone.

'The deal was for me to fix breakfast.'

'I know, but I want to so don't argue.' He kissed her swiftly. 'Now, if you keep standing there looking like that, you'll be late.'

Mariah rushed to the bathroom to take care of her morning routine. Returning to the now-vacant bedroom, she stared at the bed with its sheets tangled and the corners undone. The discarded coverlet lay in a heap on the floor near the footboard. She quickly straightened the bed, reverently running her hands where he had slept. Once the bed was restored to its neat condition, she opened the closet and yanked a scrub suit off a hanger.

Hating to give up the comfort of his soft shirt, she reluctantly let it slide off her body. No matter, she consoled herself. There was always this evening. Minutes later she walked into the kitchen.

Andrew tossed her an exasperated look. 'You don't have anything to eat. No meat, no potatoes, one egg and a half a loaf of bread.'

'I don't eat much in the morning. Why do you think I only offered you toast?' She grinned. 'If you recall, I mentioned that I hardly ever cooked. Therefore, I don't keep much food around. By the way, there's a box of cereal in the cupboard.'

He poked his head in the refrigerator and pulled out a small jug of milk. Taking a sniff, he grimaced. 'Sour. That does it.'

She watched him pour the contents down the sink. 'That does what?'

'Tonight we're staying at my place,' he said firmly. 'At least we won't starve to death.' He dropped two pieces of wholewheat bread into the toaster.

Mariah hesitated. 'I'm not sure it's a good idea.'

He regarded her with an odd look. 'Why not?'

Her mind raced as she tried to handle the situation tactfully. She poured herself a cup of coffee and clutched it in her hand. 'Remember when you told me that you didn't want anyone else in bed with us?'

The brooding lines on his face and the puzzled light in his eyes disappeared. 'Ah,' he said knowingly. 'You're worried about—'

She didn't let him finish his sentence. 'Yes.'

He moved closer to take her cup and set it on the counter. 'I haven't always slept alone.'

'You haven't?' She swallowed hard.

He shook his head and began to count on his fingers. 'First there was my brother. Once in a while, I had my two cousins. Oh, and I can't forget the times I had sleep-overs with Matt and Justin when I was a kid.'

Heat flooded her face. 'You set me up,' she accused without rancour.

He planted a swift kiss on her mouth. 'You're the first and only woman—'

The toaster popped up with a loud snap, shattering the moment as it sent the two slices of bread sailing. One landed on the countertop and the other on a waiting plate.

The action ended before they could move. Andrew stared at the offending appliance. 'What in the—?'

She giggled. 'I forgot to warn you about my catapult.'

His lopsided grin appeared and he handed her the small plate with a flourish. 'Breakfast is served.'

'You're bright-eyed and bushy-tailed,' the nursery nurse commented later that morning.

Mariah coloured, certain that everyone would guess the reason. 'It's a beautiful day.'

'That may be, but I'd enjoy it a lot more if I wasn't working this weekend,' the woman grumbled without malice. 'Why is it that the weather is gorgeous on the days I'm at the hospital, and when I'm at home it rains?'

Mariah laughed. 'Pure luck.'

'What a shock to hear about Gary.'

'It was,' Mariah agreed. 'He's a lucky man.'

'I'll say. How many people manage to be in the ER at the precise moment they need resuscitation?'

'Not many, I'm sure.' Mariah placed the heelstick blood sample in her tray and washed her hands. 'I'll call the bilirubin as soon as it's finished.'

'Thanks.'

She left the nursery with a spring to her step as Andrew occupied her thoughts. She'd never dreamed that she'd feel this way again, but she did and it was wonderful. As she rounded the corner she fell into step behind two nurses deep in a conversation.

'My money's on Kelly,' the platinum-blonde nurse declared loudly. Her comment caught Mariah's notice.

'What makes you say that?' the mousy one asked.

'Drew's known Kelly all his life. Childhood sweet-hearts, you know. A stranger can't waltz into town and break that bond.'

'You never know.'

The blonde shook her head. 'He's just using Mariah as insurance.'

'I don't follow you.'

'Simple. If Drew can't talk Kelly into staying, he has Mariah waiting in the wings. I hear they're spending a lot of time together, if you know what I mean.'

'No kidding?'

The blonde nodded. 'I have it on very good authority. In any case, the hospital will benefit from Andrew's choice. Whoever he ends up with will have a guaranteed job.'

The corridor split and the two nurses swerved to the left while Mariah travelled along the right in a state of numbness. Their speculations couldn't be true. Andrew was too sincere to inject such a cold-hearted quality into his relationships. And yet... Gossip always carried some grain of truth with it and she couldn't ignore the facts.

His interest in Mariah from the very beginning had

always hinged on Kelly. He'd taken her to dinner to persuade her to reassign Kelly to Gallup Memorial. After Mariah had refused, he'd been distant—at least until she'd complied with his wishes. Ever since then he'd been wonderful—too wonderful. Last night, or rather this morning, had been one of those occasions.

By the time she ended her shift and went home, she didn't know what to think. If the nurses had seemed mean-spirited, she could have ignored the entire incident. However, they hadn't spoken with malice and since they'd corroborated her own doubts their comments reverberated through her mind.

The only problem was what should she do?

Confronting Andrew would only bring forth a denial. The true test would be in his actions. Once he was aware of Carlie's existence, and the problems Kelly would have with her father, how he dealt with them would answer Mariah's questions.

For now she had his attention, and would make the most of the next few weeks. No matter what happened after that, this was her time. Crossing her fingers for a few uninterrupted hours after work, she rushed to the grocery store in search of lasagna ingredients. Luckily, a different clerk was on duty, saving Mariah from explaining why she was buying food staples rather than frozen dinners and sandwich fixings.

By the time Andrew returned from seeing one of his patients in the ER, she had their meal baking in the oven and a pan of brownies cooling on the counter.

'Hi,' she said, greeting him with a kiss.

He grabbed her by her waist. 'Something smells good.'

'Dinner will be ready in thirty minutes. You can relax until then.'

'Now that's good news.' He wiggled his eyebrows.

His intent was obvious. 'I know, but Jimmy Bleeker's mother called. Jimmy wants to talk to me. They'll be here any minute.'

He snapped his fingers. 'Darn.'

She laughed at his glum expression. 'Yes, well, I couldn't tell them to wait because their doctor was making a private house call, now could I?'

'I wouldn't mind.' Although his tone was offhanded, his eyes were serious and he seemed to tense.

Every sense went on alert. 'You wouldn't?'

'No.'

She didn't hesitate. 'I wouldn't either.'

Satisfaction appeared on his face. Before he could make another move, the doorbell heralded their visitors. 'Let's get rid of them as soon as possible,' he whispered in Mariah's ear. 'I'm in desperate need of TLC.'

'You're the doctor,' she whispered back. Rushing to the door, she flung it open and welcomed Mrs Bleeker and her son inside. 'Why, Jimmy, you're looking wonderful.'

'I sure am,' Jimmy said proudly. 'I wanted to thank you for Sniffles's picture. I still got it, too.' He held up the now-tattered snapshot. 'I'm gonna keep it for ever.'

'You don't know how much he depended on that picture,' Mrs Bleeker said, looking down at her son with benevolence. 'One of the nurses misplaced it while she was making his bed one morning and he was absolutely distraught until we found it again.'

'I'm glad it helped.' Mariah grabbed a brightly wrapped package off an end table. 'I made this for you, Jimmy. Sort of a glad-you're-well gift.'

Jimmy's dark eyes sparkled. 'Really?' he asked, taking the package. 'For me?'

Mariah nodded, conscious of Andrew's hand on her shoulder. 'Open it.'

He ripped the paper and lifted the lid off the flat box. 'Wow. Mom, look at this.'

Mrs Bleeker peered over his head to study the contents. A gasp escaped her and she removed the framed photo of Sniffles, staring at his young master in the hospital bed. 'It's wonderful.'

Andrew spoke in her ear. 'Remarkable evidence of my previous charge. The truth always comes out, doesn't it?'

Mariah grinned.

'Thanks, Mariah,' Jimmy said. 'I'll keep it beside my bed all the time. Will you take his picture again when he's bigger?'

'Jimmy,' his mother scolded. 'One of us can do the honours. We can't impose on Mariah again.'

'But she takes 'em the bestest,' he protested. 'She doesn't chop off people's heads or nothin'.'

Mrs Bleeker gave Mariah a wry smile. 'A family joke.'

Mariah stared at Andrew, watching his eyebrows rise in silent query. Clearly, he was interested in her answer.

Unfortunately, too many variables entered into her decision, variables that she wasn't at liberty to discuss yet.

'You know I'm only in Gallup for a short time,' she began, breaking eye contact with Andrew to look at Jimmy, 'so I can't make any promises.'

'You'll come back and visit, won't you?' the boy asked.

Once she left she wouldn't be back, but she couldn't dash a young boy's hopes. 'I'll try.'

The oven timer buzzed. 'Your dinner must be ready,' Mrs Bleeker said. 'Come, Jimmy. Let's go home.'

160   DR PRESCOTT'S DILEMMA

Moments later Mariah hurried into the kitchen to quieten the noise. Grabbing her hot pads, she carefully slid the bubbling pan of lasagna out of the oven and onto the top of the stove. 'Dinner is served,' she said brightly, hoping to divert Andrew's attention.

He paused, as if debating whether or not to continue the conversation, then said, 'Smells good.'

Throughout their meal of lasagna, salad and a loaf of French bread the conversation remained light and general. Just as Mariah let down her guard, Andrew brought up the subject she wanted to avoid.

'You're still planning to leave town?'

'I have to. When Kelly arrives my job here will be over.'

'Your job at Gallup Memorial will end,' he corrected. 'You said yourself that you could work for TLC Inc anywhere as long as you had a fax and a computer modem.'

'Yes, but I've been promoted. I'm not sure what my new responsibilities will entail.' How could she mention her fears without divulging Kelly's secret? She squared her shoulders. 'Besides, I can't ignore my other obligations, like taking care of my condo and paying my bills. I also have a dental appointment.'

'I understand all that. The question is—once you've taken care of your personal business, do you want to live in Wyoming?'

CHAPTER TEN

MARIAH'S eyes burned under Andrew's scrutiny and she rose to pace the floor. She wanted to declare her love for him, a love that had crept upon her without warning and in spite of her wishes to the contrary, but she wouldn't announce such a thing until all her doubts were gone. It would be less embarrassing, less awkward, for both of them if she waited.

'I like Gallup.'

'Then you'll return?' he pressed.

'I'm not sure. A lot can happen in the next few weeks.' After Kelly arrives, she added silently. 'We both may change our minds.'

In a flash, Andrew moved to grip her arms. 'I won't,' he said fiercely. 'No matter what.'

'No one knows what the future will hold,' she said tiredly.

His eyes lit with understanding. 'Kelly. She's what this is all about, isn't she?'

She paused, wanting to deny it but unable to do so. 'Yes.'

'Mariah, we dated for a long time, but were never officially engaged.'

'You haven't seen her for a year,' she reminded him. As he opened his mouth to speak she forestalled him. 'All I'm saying is for us to wait and see. I don't want you to make any promises that you'll regret.'

'I feel like we've had this conversation before,' he muttered, releasing her to run his hands through his hair.

She managed a tight smile. 'We have. And, like before, I don't want to rush into anything. Let's enjoy what we have today. Tomorrow will take care of itself.'

'At some point you'll have to look further ahead than your one day at a time,' he warned.

'I know.' She'd already caught herself fantasizing about long-term plans, but she immediately disregarded them as imprudent.

'OK. We'll do it your way.' He sounded resigned. 'For now.'

'If we're meant to be together, everything will work out,' she said, trying to be philosophical in the face of certain disappointment. By his own admission, he would do anything for Kelly. She also knew him well enough to know that he wouldn't ignore little Carlie.

She'd do her best to prepare for the worst—rejection—but, in the meantime, she'd enjoy their moments together to the fullest.

As if by mutual consent, they stuck to general topics while they washed the dishes. Afterwards they strolled outside to sit on the porch swing. Andrew patted the spot next to him, then flung his arm around her shoulders.

A station wagon, belonging to a family down the street, drove past and the occupants waved. Andrew smiled, then grimaced once they'd gone by. 'Much as I like this swing, there are times it's a damned nuisance.'

'Why?'

'In case you haven't noticed, we have a considerable lack of privacy.' He glanced at the ceiling. 'Maybe we could move this to the back of the house.'

'No way. That side faces west. It's too hot in the evenings.'

'There's alwa my place. The back yard is shady at this time of day.'

'If Gary's recovering from a heart attack, he doesn't need to worry about his good friend stealing his property,' she teased.

'I guess not. I'll have to buy one of my own.' He glanced at his watch. 'Chester has a band playing tonight. Want to go?'

The prospect of dancing with Andrew was extremely attractive. 'Sure. By the way, how's his dog doing?'

'Fine. The collie has taken to him like a duck to water.'

'I'm glad. Did he decide on a name?'

Andrew nodded as his mouth twitched with amusement. 'Lassie.'

Mariah punched his arm playfully. 'Chester and I are obviously on the same wavelength.'

'Well, you're both lucky. If old Lassie had been rabid, a name would have been a moot point.'

'True.' She stretched out her legs and gazed at the Latin American sandals, or huaraches, on her feet. 'I'd better slip on my dancing shoes.'

Andrew gave her a swift hug. 'You'd better—' The pager in his pocket beeped and he released her to read the message.

'I need to borrow your phone,' he said, rising.

She followed him inside. From her bedroom she heard his one-sided conversation end with, 'I'll be right there.'

He appeared in the doorway. 'One of the boys on the American Legion baseball team just got beaned on a wild throw. I'm going to check him out.'

'Want me to come along?'

He paused. 'Do you mind? I might need lab work.'

'No problem. I can wait for you in the hospital as well as here.'

Later, while she cooled her heels at the ER nurses'

station, Andrew disappeared into the trauma room. She'd finished reading a news magazine cover to cover by the time the nurse motioned to her.

'Dr Prescott needs you.'

Obviously the youth's injuries were severe. Mariah skirted the desk on her way to the cubicle. She entered and went directly to the counter where the small tray of emergency lab supplies was kept.

She approached the gurney and the teenager's parents stepped aside to allow her room. Andrew's face remained impassive but, being attuned to his moods, she recognized the concern in his eyes.

'CBC and chem-26 panel,' Andrew said quietly.

She nodded, and while she went to work he spoke to Kyle Gentry's parents. 'Has he been disoriented since it happened?'

Mrs Gentry, a woman in her late forties with obvious sunburn, answered as she clutched Kyle's right hand. 'Yes. He walked to the dugout and collapsed there. If only his helmet hadn't fallen off when he tried to steal third base. I can't believe the second baseman hit him in the head.'

Mr Gentry, a man of similar age, wearing designer sports apparel, clasped his wife's free hand. 'It was a freak accident, Lila. The important thing is for Kyle to get the best treatment.' He stared at Andrew. 'What's wrong with him, Doctor?'

'I'd say a concussion, but I'll know more after we take a few X-rays.'

'See, Mom? No big deal. I'm fine.' Kyle held a kidney basin on his chest as if he anticipated a bout of nausea.

'Vertigo, lethargy and a headache are common,' Andrew admitted. 'I'll admit him for observation.'

'Be that as it may, I want a CT scan, an MRI and a

neurologist called in,' Mr Gentry demanded. 'Admitting him for observation isn't enough. I won't have my son lying in a bed, twiddling his thumbs, while you decide if he has a skull fracture or one of those subdural things.'

Lila gasped.

'If you're referring to a subdural haematoma, I don't think that's the case,' Andrew began.

'But you won't know for sure unless you have a CT scan, right?'

'In my medical judgement—'

'You won't know for sure, will you?' he pressed.

Andrew's jaw tensed. 'No.'

Mr Gentry crossed his arms. 'Then I want one ordered immediately.'

Mariah wondered if Mr Gentry was a lawyer—he certainly had the technique of one. She struggled to keep her attention on collecting Kyle's blood, instead of on following their discussion. She was always amazed at how people tended to ignore her while she was at work. She taped a cotton ball over the pinhole in Kyle's arm, then gathered her paraphernalia together while Andrew answered Mr Gentry's command.

'It isn't that simple. We don't have the equipment or the personnel.'

'Then fly him where a scanner is available. Casper has the closest major hospital. It won't take long.'

'You're always welcome to seek out a second opinion,' Andrew said. 'However, I can't authorize a LifeWatch transfer for a non-emergency case.'

'I want the best for my son,' Mr Gentry said, his face turning red from restrained anger.

'So do I. The best you'll get is an ambulance ride.'

'Fine. But you'd better pray they don't find anything wrong because if they do, and you've refused to treat my son's injury as an emergency, I'll have your licence,' the man snapped.

Mariah froze, stunned by the man's accusation. She glanced at Andrew.

'You're welcome to try,' Andrew said, his voice even. 'Now, if you'll excuse me, I'll prepare your son's paperwork for his transfer.'

Mariah hurried from the room, a step ahead of Andrew. 'He shouldn't have said those things,' she began, wanting to encourage him.

'It's OK,' he said, reaching for the telephone on the nurses' desk. 'Just hurry with the results, will you? It shouldn't take long for an ambulance to arrive.'

Mariah hurried to the lab and began to perform the tests necessary to document Kyle's general health status. Being an active young man, she didn't expect to find anything abnormal for his age, and didn't.

She faxed the reports to ER, then closed her department and switched off the lights. Searching for Andrew, she found him where she'd left him—at the nurses' desk.

He rose, thrusting a clipboard into a slot. 'Let's go.'

She glanced around. The ER seemed quiet, almost eerie. 'Where's your patient?'

'On his way to the hospital at Casper. The doctor will call me once they have the result of his CT scan.'

Sensing his pensive mood, she didn't push for conversation. At home he sank onto his recliner as he flexed his shoulders. Without a word, she moved behind him and began to knead the tension out of his muscles. Her hands warmed from the friction of her palms against his cotton shirt and from his body heat.

After fifteen minutes of silence he spoke. 'That was all so unnecessary.'

She moved her hands to massage his temples. 'How so?'

'If we had a CT scanner on site, I could have checked Kyle out myself.'

'Yes, but we don't.' She hesitated, trying to frame her question tactfully. 'Do you think you made a mistake in Kyle Gentry's diagnosis?'

His 'no' was vehement. 'Although it would have been nice to show his father the evidence.'

'Mr Gentry strikes me as the type of man who wouldn't believe the data, anyway. At least not unless he had two other opinions to confirm it.'

'You're right,' he said, clearly dispirited.

'As for a CT scanner, you'll get one. I have confidence in you. Once you bring more doctors to town the demand will be greater and the hospital will have to accommodate the need.' She flung her arms around his neck and trailed her hands down his chest.

'In a few years you'll have made so many changes that people won't recognize the place. New doctors, more staff, extra wings to house the extra diagnostic equipment—you name it, it will be here. Gallup will be the medical centre for this part of the state.'

Andrew turned to stare at her, laughter appearing in his eyes. 'Reaching for the stars, aren't you?'

She shrugged. 'Why not? You know what you want and you're stubborn enough to go after it.'

He raised one eyebrow. 'Stubborn, eh?'

'Persevering and tenacious,' she corrected, smiling.

'That's better,' he said, sounding more lighthearted. Before she could respond he tugged her onto his lap. 'You know something?'

Mariah stared into his eyes, happy to see the strain lessening. 'No, what?'

'You're good for my ego, Ms Henning.'

'Just your ego?' She pretended affront.

He shook his head. 'No. For me. I think I'll keep you.' As he kissed her she hoped he'd feel the same way in a few weeks.

Long after Mariah went to work early on Sunday morning, and at a more convenient hour for the nursing staff, Andrew made his rounds and took a call from the Gentry boy's doctor. They'd found no evidence of a fracture or a haematoma.

Once he returned home his house seemed lonely in spite of Mariah's lingering scent. Reading the latest medical journals didn't appeal to him, but physical labour did.

As per Andrew's instructions, a friend had started to build a wooden fence to enclose his back yard. Since he was working on Andrew's project in his spare time, the finished product was slow in coming. The supporting posts had finally been cemented into the ground and the crossbars bolted into place. All that remained was for someone to nail the boards vertically onto the horizontal beams.

It was one of those jobs that if interrupted wouldn't ruin the entire project. It seemed like the perfect therapy to while away the hours. With luck, it would also cure his edginess and frustration over Mariah's cautious nature.

He aligned the boards with the top plumb line and began pounding nails. For the first few he concentrated on his task. Then, as he established a routine, his thoughts drifted back to Mariah. Wanting to make plans for their future, he knew that patience was necessary. For some reason, Mariah continued to believe that his feelings for her would change once Kelly arrived on the scene, and nothing he said would convince her of his sincerity.

His heart wouldn't be swayed because he loved her as he'd never loved a woman before in his life.

It also didn't help his cause when people in town persisted in linking his name with Kelly's. The gossips of Gallup had added fuel to the fires of Mariah's doubts and all Andrew could do to counteract the flames was to wait.

He'd heard about the betting pool concerning Mariah and Kelly, and if he'd caught wind of it then Mariah had also. The idea irritated him no end. Obviously Gallup needed more interesting activity if the spotlight of community concern rested on his love life.

He pounded a final nail into the rough cedar plank, before moving to another board.

In spite of his eagerness, he understood her reluctance to look ahead. She'd planned a future once before and had then watched those dreams die. Gary's sudden illness hadn't helped matters either. Her leeriness was natural and expected, but it didn't make his life easier. Perhaps Gary's positive outcome would sway her opinion.

He faced a waiting game, a game he didn't like to play. While brooding over circumstances, the hammer glanced off the nail head and he hit his thumb. He muffled a curse as he inspected for damage. Finding none, he returned to his self-imposed labour.

As he fell into a steady rhythm his thoughts wandered again. Ever since he'd seen signs of depression in Virginia Evers, he'd tried everything to convince Kelly to return. Mariah's presence had seemed heaven-sent in achieving his objective. However, accomplishing his goal had come at the expense of losing Mariah. He didn't like the price tag.

Mariah enjoyed her job at TLC and it showed in the way she referred to it. Quitting wasn't an option. He simply wanted her to work out of Gallup rather than Denver. For her to make such a decision, however, she had to be convinced that he looked upon Kelly as a friend and not a romantic interest. His reassurances hadn't done the trick and his lack of success frustrated him.

Some might call him a glutton for punishment, others might describe him as foolish for not giving up in the face of obvious failure. Yet he couldn't. Good things never came easy and he believed she was the best thing ever to come into his life. Mariah was worth fighting for.

Being fond of photography, she was clearly one of those people who had to 'see' rather than 'hear' in order to believe. He'd bide his time until Mariah saw for herself that he hadn't spoken empty words.

The cell phone, lying on the stack of lumber, jingled and as he answered he heard Bonnie's terse voice. 'The county EMS called us. They're bringing two victims from a car accident.'

He instantly forgot the pain in his thumb. 'How bad?'

'Internal injuries, broken bones, lacerations. I've alerted our surgical staff, radiology and lab.'

'I'm on my way.'

He arrived in ER ahead of the ambulance. He waited on the loading dock and helped the emergency medical technicians unload their human cargo. As he bent over the woman on the stretcher—noting her bruised and bloodied face, her body bundled to a backboard, her neck immobilized with a cervical collar—he recognized her as Virginia Evers. His heart sank to his stomach.

Mariah hovered in the corner of Trauma One, ready to spring into action at the word of Andrew or the surgeon, Dr Markham. The name of her patients startled her more than the sight of their injuries.

Winston and Virginia Evers.

Fate obviously wasn't being kind to the citizens of Gallup this weekend.

She listened to Andrew's authoritative orders, hearing him call out instructions for X-rays, IVs and drugs. Winston was wheeled into the second station in the same room, loudly proclaiming his concern for his wife.

Finally, Andrew motioned Mariah forward. 'CBC, cross-match for two units, electrolytes. We'll be taking Virginia to surgery for a splenectomy so I also want four units of packed red cells and two units of platelets available.'

By the time she'd finished drawing Virginia's blood he had decided on a CBC, chemistry profile, and X-rays of Winston's thigh and hip. A few minutes later, just as she was leaving with the necessary blood samples in hand, Andrew drew her aside. She met his troubled dark gaze, bracing herself for the inevitable.

'Kelly's their next-of-kin. She has to be called home,' he said grimly. 'Today.'

CHAPTER ELEVEN

MARIAH stared at the page on her lap in an attempt to read the letter written on a TLC Inc letterhead, but her concentration was non-existent. Each time the automatic entrance doors whooshed open she scrutinized the new arrival in the hope—and fear—it would be Kelly.

'I've been looking for you,' Andrew said, sinking onto one of the chairs beside her. 'I heard you hadn't left.'

'I've been waiting for Kelly. She said to expect her around eight and it's half past.'

A furrow appeared in his forehead. 'The receptionist can tell her where to find her parents. It isn't necessary for you to stay.'

She shrugged, unwilling to explain her reason for lingering in the lobby. The reason would be obvious once Kelly arrived with Carlie. Six-month-old babies weren't welcome visitors in the hospital, and she had volunteered to watch Carlie while Kelly saw her parents.

'How are Virginia and Winston?'

'They're both stable. Markham removed Virginia's spleen, but she'll be OK. Winston is already worrying about who will take care of his livestock. Between Kelly and the neighbours, they'll look after them.' He tipped her chin upward. 'You're tired.'

'Gee, thanks. Just what I wanted to hear.' She shrugged. 'It's been a stressful weekend.' Both physically and mentally, she thought.

'I'll wait for Kelly. Go home.'

'In a few minutes,' she temporized. 'Shouldn't you be making rounds or something?' The reunion of Kelly and Andrew after a year's absence was inevitable, but Mariah would rather not observe the occasion. It was bound to be more touching than she could handle.

The doors whooshed open again. This time Mariah recognized the young woman who was entering the hospital with a baby in her arms and a diaper bag slung over one shoulder. With dread filling her mouth, she rose as stiffly as an arthritic person, leaving her sheaf of papers on the chair she'd vacated.

She stole a glance at Andrew. The lines in his face had softened at the sight of the petite strawberry-blonde.

'Drew!' Kelly's face whitened as she froze. Then, after a tentative step forward, she rushed towards him, dropping the bag in her haste.

Mariah watched Andrew meet Kelly halfway, hugging her close. Not a platonic hug either, she thought with a sinking sensation in her stomach. And certainly not like the consoling hug he'd given Tricia Wright.

Kelly was crying, probably from joy, while Mariah's own misery threatened to display itself. She blinked rapidly to stop the burning behind her eyelids. Her doubts about Andrew's feelings for Kelly fled—this emotional meeting spoke for itself. Carlie's identity would be the crowning touch in restoring their relationship.

She inched her way forward, wishing that she could walk through the door, hop into her car and head for Denver.

Squeezed between Andrew and her mother, young

Carlie, a miniature replica of her mother, squealed her displeasure and interrupted Kelly's embrace.

'Oh, Mariah,' Kelly said, her voice thick with emotion as she leaned against Andrew. 'I'm so glad you're here.' She kissed Carlie's temple, before handing her to Mariah. 'Mommy will see you in a little while.'

'Mommy?' Andrew asked, his features puzzled.

Mariah exchanged a glance with Kelly. Kelly straightened her shoulders and faced Andrew. 'Carlie is my daughter.'

If the situation hadn't been so serious, Mariah might have laughed at his befuddled expression. But it was, and so she didn't. 'Your daughter?' he asked, incredulous.

'Yes.

His eyes narrowed as he faced Kelly. 'How old is she?'

'Six months.'

He glanced at Mariah. 'You knew?'

Although he didn't add, 'and didn't tell me?' she read the question in his eyes. Unable to find her voice, Mariah nodded.

'Then she's—'

Mariah winced, waiting for him to say 'mine'. Instead, Kelly interrupted. 'I'd rather discuss it later, Drew. After I see my folks and at a place where we'll have more privacy.' She pointedly glanced around the lobby.

'I'll take her home,' Mariah said. 'I live in the house across from Andrew.'

'Thanks.' Kelly stared up at Andrew. 'It's good to see you again, although I wish it had been under better circumstances.'

He gave Mariah an I'll-talk-to-you-later look, before smiling down on Kelly. 'Your parents are doing fine. I'll take you to them.'

Jealousy surged through Mariah, but she didn't have time to dwell on her feelings. Carlie was squirming in her arms and demanding attention. 'Ready for bed, half-pint?' she asked, heading for the exit.

After warming a bottle of formula for Carlie and rocking her to sleep, Mariah placed the child on her bed. While Carlie squirmed herself into a comfortable position with her bottom in the air, Mariah surrounded her with folded blankets and pillows to prevent an untimely roll onto the floor. Her protective measures in place, Mariah turned the lights low and sat in the dark living room.

For the next hour she reviewed her options. Leaving seemed the cowardly thing to do, but she really didn't have a choice. Kelly would take her place at the lab and, from all indications, she would do the same in Andrew's personal life. He'd said himself that he would do anything for her. There would be nothing left for Mariah in Gallup.

By eleven o'clock Kelly still hadn't arrived and Mariah dozed in her chair. When she next awoke the clock read one a.m. As she padded across the floor to lock the door she noticed a soft light burning in Andrew's picture window and his Land Cruiser parked in the driveway.

Obviously Andrew and Kelly were catching up on old times and a fresh burst of pain pierced her heart. In the next instant she made her decision. She would leave Gallup at the first available opportunity.

'I'm sorry I hurt you, Drew,' Kelly began, 'but I didn't
have a choice. You know my father as well as I do.'

'You should have told me,' he chided.

Tears came to her eyes and she traced the design on
the sofa cushion. 'I couldn't. You've always been so
wonderful to me. I didn't have the courage to tell you
that I loved you like a best friend and not as a lover. I
thought it would be enough, but I wanted the sparks, the
fireworks, the bells and whistles.'

'And did you find them with Slade?'

'I thought so but...' she grimaced '...he fooled me.
The sparks fizzled out. He left town the day I told him
I was pregnant.'

'So you made plans to leave.'

She nodded. 'I didn't want to embarrass you and my
conscience wouldn't let me trick you into believing that
Carlie was your child. I never was good at keeping secrets, which is why I didn't stay in touch with anyone.'

'Your strategy worked because I didn't have a clue.
Mariah never breathed a word and, believe me, if I'd
known I wouldn't have been so hard on her at first.'

He shook his head, wincing at the harsh words he'd
spoken out of ignorance. She could have saved herself
anguish if she'd mentioned Kelly's situation. Yet she'd
braved his wrath rather than sacrifice loyalty. If he
hadn't fallen in love with her before, he would now.

'I'd have been happy to claim Carlie as mine,' he
added, as an afterthought.

She touched his arm. 'I know. You've always bailed
me out of my scrapes, but I couldn't let you do it again.
This time I had to save myself.'

'Did you?'

Kelly nodded. 'I have a good job, a wonderful daughter and someday I'll find someone special, like you did with Mariah.'

'Was I so obvious?' he asked, twisting his mouth into a wry grin.

'Not at first,' she admitted. 'But, after seeing the crushed look on her face when I went straight to you—and after hearing you mention her name all evening—I've drawn my own conclusions.'

He grinned. 'What can I say? I love her.'

Kelly hugged him. 'I've always wanted the best for you, Drew. I'm glad you've finally found it.'

Now if only he could keep it from slipping through his fingers.

Kelly strode into the lab the next afternoon with a frown. 'I have a problem, Mariah.'

Mariah's fingers slowed as she cleaned the stage of the microscope. Her heart leaped into her throat and her mind raced with unspeakable thoughts. 'Professional or personal?'

'Professional.'

She relaxed her guard. If Andrew had been part of Kelly's problem, she couldn't possibly give sound advice.

'I should go back to Sheridan as the girl they've hired won't start for two more weeks,' Kelly admitted. 'However, I don't feel comfortable leaving my parents right now. I know they're in the hospital and I can't do much, but...'

'Let me guess,' Mariah said. 'You'd rather be in Gallup than finish your term in Sheridan.'

Kelly nodded, her face sheepish. 'Yes. Do you have someone available who can fill in for me? It seems like a waste of time to send someone for a few weeks, but the clinic is desperate and I hate to leave them in the lurch.'

Mariah had already anticipated such a request, although she was glad Kelly had mentioned it first. She'd been searching for a solution all morning. 'I'll work something out.'

Kelly's relief was palpable. 'Would you?'

'I'll check my schedules and juggle things a bit, but don't worry. If this is what you want, I'll iron out the details.'

'You're the greatest,' Kelly exclaimed.

Mariah grinned. 'Please keep your opinion to yourself. I don't want to ruin my ruthless businesswoman reputation. If Nancy doesn't object to the change then neither do I.' She motioned Nancy to join them.

'With my parents in the hospital, I'd like to begin on Monday,' Kelly told the other tech. 'They won't need my help as such until they're discharged.'

'Would that arrangement satisfy you?' Mariah asked.

Nancy nodded. 'I didn't get the chance to tell you yesterday but, by some quirk of fate, the human resources office received two applications in the mail. Both techs have agreed to join us within the month.' She addressed Kelly. 'If your parents go home before these two start maybe you can help on a part-time basis.'

'Sure. No problem,' Kelly said. 'Andrew said if I got everything worked out, he'd move my things this weekend—that is if you don't mind, Mariah.'

The news caught Mariah by surprise. Obviously he'd

forgotten his intention to fill *her* weekend. Feeling Nancy's gaze rest on her, she managed to speak in an even tone. 'Not at all. I'm glad he's available. It's tough to organize everything with a baby in tow.' Self-preservation forced her to change the subject. 'What did your parents think of Carlie?'

Kelly's eyes shone. 'Mom's absolutely delighted. Drew says the prospect of playing with her granddaughter will speed her recovery. Dad hasn't said too much—he's disappointed I'm not married—but Drew thinks he won't resist her charm for long.'

Hearing Andrew's name casually interspersed in Kelly's conversation set Mariah's teeth on edge. 'I'm sure he's right.' Speaking with a false sense of gaiety, she rose. 'Since we have Gallup Memorial's contract worked out to everyone's satisfaction, I'll see if I can make our other client equally happy.'

As Kelly had predicted, the administrator of the Sheridan Medical Clinic was in dire straits for a lab person. Luckily, he understood Kelly's desire to be with her family and agreed that another tech would take her place.

Mariah volunteered, considering TLC's lack of available techs as providential. From the way Kelly quoted Andrew's every word, it was only a matter of time before wedding bells rang. Watching them rekindle their romance was more than she could contemplate and, luckily, the perfect means to avoid the ordeal had fallen into her lap.

Even the timing was perfect. Their moving day would coincide and, figuratively speaking, she and Andrew would go their separate ways. After Friday she would make a fresh start once again.

Why did the idea hurt so much?

Tired of packing, Mariah took time that evening to sit outside and enjoy the Wyoming summer weather. Across the street Andrew's fence was taking shape. At the same time she noticed that his Land Cruiser was gone.

To her surprise, his front door opened and he strode toward her house. Dread filled her soul. Ever since Kelly had stayed at Andrew's until the wee hours of the morning, presumably to work out their battered relationship, Mariah had been waiting for his rejection speech and had done everything she could to delay the inevitable.

As he bounded up the porch steps he appeared tired, but wore a welcoming smile.

'I didn't think you were home,' she said.

'Kelly borrowed my truck.' He sank onto a chair. 'You're a hard woman to contact. I tried nearly all day. Didn't you get my messages?'

Mariah continued to rock the porch swing with one bare foot on the concrete and the other tucked underneath her. 'I've been on the phone most of the day.'

'Kelly's moving this weekend.'

'So she said.' Mariah hid her inner turmoil behind a front of cool indifference.

'Want to come along?'

It took her a moment to assimilate his unexpected invitation. 'What?'

'Do you want to come along?' he repeated.

She was astonished at his request. 'Sorry. I'll be busy.'

A puzzled line appeared on his forehead. 'I didn't know you'd made plans for the weekend.'

'I hadn't until today. I'm going to Sheridan, then home to Denver.' She drew a deep breath. 'I won't be back.' Speaking past the lump in her throat, she hadn't realized how hard it would be to say those two words. She uncoiled her leg and rose. 'If you'll excuse me, I'm in the middle of packing.'

Before she could sweep regally past him, Andrew grabbed her elbow and stopped her in her tracks. 'You can't drop that bombshell and walk away. What's going on?'

She stared at him in amazement. 'Kelly's replacing me. If you'll recall, that was the arrangement.'

'The *arrangement*—' he stressed the word '—was for Kelly to take over on August fifteenth. According to my calendar, that's two weeks away.'

'Our agreement was for Kelly to arrive when she was available, at which time I would leave. She's available.'

'I thought she wasn't finished with the clinic in Sheridan.'

'She's not. I'm taking her place.'

Andrew stared into her eyes. 'Dammit, Mariah. I want those two weeks.'

She shrugged. She'd wanted them as well, but it was pointless to bemoan what wasn't possible. 'In case you've forgotten, I'm trying to run a business,' she said in her most professional tone. 'Kelly's here because of her family emergency. What would you have me do? Send her to Sheridan to fulfil the letter of her contract, or switch places with her so she'll be available to give her parents the emotional support they need?'

He didn't answer.

'Well? Which option should I have chosen?' she demanded.

His shoulders slumped, as if he clearly recognized her dilemma.

She wrenched her arm out of his grip. 'I've done everything possible, short of moving heaven and earth, to meet your demands so I don't want to hear any complaints. You know the saying about being careful what you wish for because you might get it. Well, Andrew, I gave you your wish. If you don't like it don't blame me.' She ended her speech on a quivery note.

For a long moment he didn't speak. Finally, he released her. 'Why won't you come back?'

She drew a shaky breath. 'It's not a good idea.'

'Says who?' he demanded.

'You and Kelly need time to explore your feelings.'

'There's nothing to explore,' he ground out. 'We had a long visit last night. She's a close friend, nothing more.'

Mariah leaned against the porch railing. 'Are you sure? When you laid eyes on Kelly you two didn't greet each other like long-lost friends.'

'So I was a little enthusiastic. The minute I kissed her, though, I knew she wasn't the woman for me.' His voice softened. 'You are.'

She'd wanted to hear those words and yet... 'I'd like to believe you, but I can't.'

His expression was explosive as he ran one hand along the back of his neck. 'For a woman who has a wonderful talent for looking beneath the surface when you take photographs, you're not able to do the same in our situation.'

'I beg your pardon,' she said hotly. 'I have looked beneath the surface and guess what I found? I saw a man who can't seem to make up his mind. First you want Kelly, then you claim you want me. When will you change your mind again?'

'I know what I want, Mariah,' he said quietly. 'It may have taken me a while to realize it, but I've made my final decision. In fact, I made it a long time ago. I love you.'

'So you say.'

He looked down at her, incredulous. 'I don't know what sort of man you're used to, but making love isn't something I take lightly.'

She'd sensed that, but evidence suggested otherwise. 'What about Carlie?'

His brow furrowed. 'What about her?'

'How can you say that about your own daughter?' she asked, astounded.

His jaw dropped, then closed. His eyes widened and he blinked owlishly. 'My...what?'

'Carlie. Your daughter,' she said impatiently. 'Or have you forgotten her already?'

Andrew shook his head. 'Carlie isn't my daughter.'

Her heart seemed to stop and time seemed to stand still. 'She isn't?'

His shocked expression gave way to one of comprehension. 'No wonder you never believed me when I said that Kelly and I were only friends.'

Mariah's mind could only focus on one thing. 'She really and truly isn't your daughter?'

He held up his hand, as if swearing a courtroom oath. 'Really and truly. Carlie's father is a man by the name of Slade Michaels. He worked for Kelly's dad for a few months before he moved to so-called greener pastures.'

'Oh, my gosh.' Mariah hid her face in her hands. 'I'm so embarrassed. Kelly told me a long time ago the reason behind her decision to leave Gallup. As you two were engaged, I assumed—'

'Wrong,' he finished. 'You should have asked me.'

'I couldn't, not after Kelly had taken such pains to hide the fact. Besides, it wasn't any of my business. After I met Virginia Evers, though, I knew their family needed some impetus to get back together. So I did my part.'

'So *that's* why you changed your mind about Kelly filling our contract.'

Mariah nodded. 'I saw how much love you have to give someone. Your daughter deserved a portion.'

'I appreciate your motives,' he said wryly, 'even if they were misguided.'

'You also told me that you'd help Kelly if she was in trouble,' she reminded him.

'I still would. But I draw the line at marriage.'

She had another concern on her mind. 'I thought you were nice to me because I'd agreed to send Kelly home.'

'Like I said before, I wanted her here because her mother needed her. I'd begun to question my opinion of you and your decision simply proved to me how wrong I'd been. I wanted to get to know you.' His gaze grew intent. 'Now that we've cleared up all those sordid details, will you come back to Gallup? To me?'

Her brain could hardly take in her good fortune. The future seemed too good to be true and she said so.

His voice softened to a caress. 'Don't complicate the issue. We love each other, but nothing comes with a guarantee. You're a part of me, whether you want to believe it or not. We might have two years together or fifty, but I want that time with you. I'm not letting you run away from me.'

Her lingering doubts and fears disintegrated. 'I love you, Andrew,' she said softly, 'so I won't run any more. I'll be back, complicating your life as usual.'

He drew her into his arms. 'Those weren't complications—they were blessings in disguise.'

EPILOGUE

DR ANDREW PRESCOTT slipped off his black tuxedo jacket and flung it around his bride's shoulders as protection from the late September air before they sneaked out of Gallup's Community Center and into his waiting Land Cruiser.

'I thought we'd never get away. What a madhouse,' he exclaimed after he slid behind the wheel and fought through the ruffles and lace of Mariah's gown to find the ignition.

'But a nice one,' she said.

He stepped on the gas and the vehicle shot into the street. 'Kelly and Becky are running interference for us. The whole town is packed inside.'

'It's a big day when the town's most eligible bachelor joins the married ranks,' she teased her husband of four hours. 'I can't believe we planned our wedding in six weeks.'

'Considering I've hardly seen you during that time, I can,' he grumbled, good-naturedly.

Mariah smiled, remembering the past month. She'd utilized her time at Sheridan to iron out the details of handling her new TLC duties in Gallup. Glenn Howell had agreed that his new vice-president could accomplish her duties out of her home, based on the fact she'd done so for the previous weeks.

Andrew had met her at the clinic as her final shift had

ended and they'd spent the weekend in Denver, clearing out her condo. She'd given away everything she didn't want and the two of them rented a truck to carry the remainder of her belongings to Gallup.

The details of her life had fallen into place and now Mariah looked forward to having Andrew to herself for their Canadian honeymoon.

Andrew pulled into his drive, then escorted her to the front entrance. Surprising her in a quick move, she found herself resting against his chest while he carried her over the threshold and slammed the door with his foot.

He set her on her feet, both hands circling her waist. 'Would you like to see your wedding present, Mrs Prescott?'

'Oh, Andrew. You shouldn't have.'

'Actually, it's for both of us.' He led her through the dining room, stood in front of the glass patio door and pointed outside. 'What do you think?'

Her hands flew to her cheeks as she gazed on her gift. 'It's beautiful.' Tears shimmered in her eyes as she studied her husband. 'Thank you.'

'We should get a few weeks' use out of it before winter hits,' he said.

'I certainly hope so.'

Outside, suspended from the support beams and freshly painted white, hung an old-fashioned porch swing.

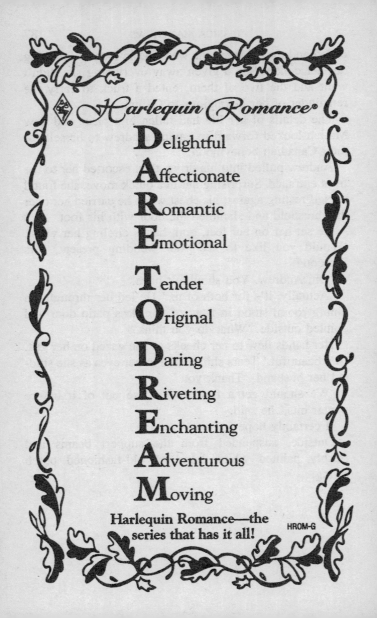

HARLEQUIN ◆ PRESENTS®

HARLEQUIN PRESENTS
men you won't be able to resist
falling in love with...

HARLEQUIN PRESENTS
women who have feelings
just like your own...

HARLEQUIN PRESENTS
powerful passion in
exotic international settings...

HARLEQUIN PRESENTS
intense, dramatic stories that will keep you
turning to the very last page...

HARLEQUIN PRESENTS
The world's bestselling romance series!

Harlequin® Historical

**From rugged lawmen and
valiant knights to defiant heiresses
and spirited frontierswomen,
Harlequin Historicals will
capture your imagination with
their dramatic scope, passion
and adventure.**

**Harlequin Historicals…
they're too good to miss!**

LOOK FOR OUR FOUR FABULOUS MEN!

Each month some of today's bestselling authors bring
four new fabulous men to Harlequin American Romance.
Whether they're rebel ranchers, millionaire power brokers
or sexy single dads, they're all gallant princes—and
they're all ready to sweep you into lighthearted fantasies
and contemporary fairy tales where anything is possible
and where all your dreams come true!

You don't even have to make a wish…
Harlequin American Romance will grant your every desire!

Look for Harlequin American Romance
wherever Harlequin books are sold!